Black Rose Days

Black Rose Days

Martin Malone

NEW ISLAND

BLACK ROSE DAYS
First published in 2016 by
New Island Books
16 Priory Office Park
Stillorgan
Co. Dublin
Republic of Ireland

www.newisland.ie

Print ISBN: 978-1-84840-517-2
Epub ISBN: 978-1-84840-518-9
Mobi ISBN: 978-1-84840-519-6

British Library Cataloguing Data.
A CIP catalogue record for this book is available from the British Library.

Typeset by JVR Creative India
Cover Design by Karen Vaughan
Printed by ScandBook AB, Sweden

10 9 8 7 6 5 4 3 2 1

Praise for Martin Malone

'Martin Malone writes stories of profound originality. He has a great sense of history and how it can be made special for a modern reader. His work searches out the spirit and language of many countries, and it is enticing from the first sentence … a writer to watch.' – *Stand UK*

'Like Carver he brings us the blue-collar experience and he tells it in the same minimalist fashion – staccato sentences and very few frills… He is a storyteller first.' – *The Sunday Times*

'Malone excels in his natural ability to tell a story, to draw readers in and hold them there.' – *Books Ireland*

Praise for Us

'With its themes of incest, suicide, and general, horrible dysfunction, at times *Us* resembles a less-sickening version of Iain Banks' *The Wasp Factory* [...] This is ultimately a distinctly Irish book – and a very good one too. Anyone interested in discovering the mundane yet freakish realities of Ireland today (albeit as seen through a very dark filter) should read it.' – *Irish American Post*

'This is a vital and readable book which highlights once again the guilt and denial endemic in our society.' – *Evening Herald*

'Powerful, disturbing and profoundly moving.' – *The Good Book Guide*

'A human story told with real emotion and sensitivity … Malone brings this story to life with an insight and understanding as only one who has been there can … an excellent read.' – *Morning Star, UK*

'A traditional Irish story with occasional stunning images.' – *The Irish Times*

'Extraordinarily accomplished and beautifully realised.' – *Irish Examiner*

'There are no corny lines here – Malone's humour being of the pitch black variety.' – *Sunday Tribune*

Also by Martin Malone

Novels
Valley of the Peacock Angel
The Only Glow of the Day
The Silence of the Glasshouse
The Broken Cedar (*IMPAC nominated*)
After Kafra
Us

Short Stories
The Mango War & Other Stories
Deadly Confederacies

Radio Plays
The Devil's Garden
Song of the Small Bird
Rosanna Nightwalker

Stage
Rosanna Nightwalker

Non-Fiction
The Lebanon Diaries

About the Author

Martin Malone is an Irish novelist and short story writer. His novel *The Broken Cedar* was nominated for the 2003 International IMPAC Dublin Literary Award. *Us* won the John B. Keane/*Sunday Independent* Award and his short story, 'The Mango War', won the RTÉ Francis MacManus Award in 2004. Martin's work has also won the Killarney International Short Story Prize and was twice shortlisted for both a Hennessy Award and a P. J. O'Connor Award. Martin worked as a military policeman with the Irish Army, under the flag of the United Nations. He served five tours of duty in Lebanon and one in Iraq.

1

Ena is what they call me but I grew up being called Mena, and to be honest I always preferred Mena. It's as if I've been two different people in my life: Ena and Mena. Things were better for me when I was a kid, before stuff started to happen. Age seven, I would say, is when my head started to go all over the place. Something must have happened to trigger the switch from Mena to Ena, or so a mind doctor said more or less to himself, after I'd cut myself that first time. I told him ... eventually ... what I thought it might be, but first he had to come at me with little loads of questions – and each one for him must have been like tilling a rocky garden with a surgeon's knife.

I used to have long beautiful red hair and I was always so skinny, with small curves, even after I started working in the chipper's that I never really liked working in.... But we needed the money and lots of people have to do things they dread doing. I loved the free takeaway that Luigi used to give me at going-home time. He made a big deal out of the act, as if he was taking it out of his very heart. He wasn't Italian or anything – it was just a nickname people stuck to him. He didn't even look Italian, though he used to say he'd been in Rome and had met Pope Whoever.

Another guy called Young Benny – he was thirty – used to work behind the counter too. He was nice. But if he didn't like the look of you, he could be mean. Once he put a slug in a bag of chips because the woman buying them never used to say please or thanks when he served her – he said that was the reason, but I think it was because of how she'd looked at him. Not just him, us, like our being alive was a sign that God was slipping up. Experimenting with creation, like. She wasn't a bad woman, not really. She baked buns when my Granny Terri died and brought them over and told my mother if she wanted anything doing, just to let her know. Still, I couldn't run out of Luigi's and up to her about the slug. Benny must have seen something in my expression for he said not to worry, that the vinegar would kill the slug – and that the French ate them until they were slithering out of their holes, and none of them ever died from the experience. The French, he said, not the slugs. He laughed after he said that, shook his head, as though surprised by his own wit.

You had to like Young Benny, with the flesh birthmark in the middle of his forehead, because I don't believe he cared what people thought, except for those who thought badly of him without reason.

I was fifteen when I started to do occasional work in Luigi's takeaway. It used be across from the wallpaper factory so he got the custom from the workers there and the kids in the three local schools. I only worked there a couple of evenings during the week in the beginning as he wanted to train me in when it wasn't so busy. Couldn't work full-time anyway as I was too young and still going to the College of Mickey Dodgers as he used to call it, laughing and thinking it hilariously funny, like he was the first to think up the name. I'd say he was wrong by about a hundred years. Never occurred to me that he shouldn't be speaking like that to a girl not yet sixteen.

Mammy used to look at me funny in those days. I think she saw the change in me, the slide from Mena into Ena. I was the oldest and she had a boy and a girl after me, but not from the same man. I should have had another brother but he only lived for a day – got enough gulps of air and a feel of the world and thought he'd gotten off at Hell. And took the last breath out of there. Couldn't blame him, really. Not knowing you're dead, not knowing you're anything, is probably better than knowing you're alive … sometimes, at any rate.

Daddy, mine, often came and went. He didn't like to hang around places where he felt people needed him. He used to be a pro boxer and was from Manchester where he had another wife and family, which we didn't find out about until his funeral. Rained so hard that Monday afternoon, rain I'd never seen the likes of before or since. Rain that wasn't content with just drowning you, but wanted to stab hard at you. Half-sisters and half-brothers cried for their father. I didn't. I think he preferred us to them, seeing as he wanted to be buried in our local cemetery. Or maybe he made the decision because Granny Terri had already bought the plot and there was no sense in wasting money on another. He could be practical when he wasn't being a bollix.

Mammy had a short fuse and Daddy out of badness used to do things to light her gale – like whenever he struck a match to light the fire or the gas ring, he would blow it out and put it back in the box, knowing Mammy would spend ages picking out loads of spent matches. Or he would hawk up phlegm from the depth of himself and push it around his mouth for an age before spitting into the kitchen sink. A sink that when he was drunk he used to wash his willy in, so Mammy had said. I had never seen that happen, but did sometimes get a smell of piss and Dettol from the plughole.

A ton of undiluted shite, Mammy said of him. Yet she cried buckets at his funeral – with a second wife and his other kids.

Once, I had sat on the sofa armrest, leaning into Daddy with his arm draped around me. It was summer and I was in shorts and my legs were brown and scraped here and there from climbing trees and fighting with the boys. He smelled of sour beer from the night before. I didn't like his smell, but I wanted to be close to him and so put up with it. We were watching telly. A Donald Duck cartoon – he was my favourite Disney character – I loved his cackling voice and how mad he used to get. Sunday afternoon, the cartoon ended, and he placed his hand on my thigh and squeezed gently, looked at me for what I thought was a long time – the longest time ever. Suddenly he pushed me away, told me to go clean my room; it was a pigsty. I didn't know what I had done that turned him to ice, but later it came to me what the pushing away was all about.

Mammy was extremely put out that Daddy had another wife, and naturally, we were too. We were shocked he could do such a thing, and amazed. For someone who spoke a lot, he'd never let a morsel of a clue slip from his mouth. A fat man who used to be a boxer, like I said, flat nose and cauliflower ears and a puffiness over his eyebrows that always seemed as if they were swellings that never fully went down.

He hit me once, when he was drunk. On the upper arm. The pain lasted an age and the bruise for weeks. Forget what it was about, though I have a slight memory of it being over something smart that I might have said to Mammy. Though it could have been over nothing.

Nothing to us, that is, not to him. He must have had some reason, I used think. Now I know that there are some people who just like to hurt others for no reason.

When I was little, maybe seven, I began to run cross-country. A mile from the estate where we lived was the Curragh Plains and a crowd of us little ones would walk the mile out there and change in the furze bushes and train. I hated it. The plains looked so vast – there was sheep dirt and thistles and patches of marsh and a fox covert where the silage men dumped the waste they collected from the people not connected to the main sewage system. They called it the Curragh Plains but it wasn't really a plain, because there were small hills on it. I only went out there a few times. Allowing thorns to stick into the soles of my feet and smashing heel-first into sheep droppings wasn't my thing. I did play hide-and-seek out there when I got older – that was fun. Used to watch the racehorses galloping. Sometimes their riders would shout at us and crack jokes among themselves. I'm sure now, looking back, that they said some dirty things – the sort of laughter they used, it became familiar to my ears.

What might have killed Mena and made me Ena, I think, is the day I was uptown with Mammy. It was wet and extremely windy and very cold. I had the sniffles bad and a chill along the full length of my spine. But Mammy said I was the least sickest child in the house and she needed my face beside her, so as to encourage the shopkeeper to extend us a little more slate. He might refuse her, but not me, not if I looked up at him with what she called 'those angelic eyes'.

So we went up the hill. It was windy and the wind was blowing this way and that, like it was lost and looking for a signpost, a pointer, for where to go. Spits of rain blew against my face. The cold was bringing a sharp axe to my bones. So cold I peed myself. Mammy's hand tight around mine, strangling my little fingers, hurting them. The wind pushed hard into our faces, as though it was trying to stop us

5

from being somewhere. Reaching the footpath at the corner of a pub, we stopped and waited for a break in the traffic so as to cross the road. An old woman called Bella Foster was beside us. She used to teach Irish dancing in the convent. She knew us to see but pretended she didn't. She tried to keep her woolly hat on her head and her cloth shopping bag from blowing away. She was tiny and skinny and I overheard later that at one time she was very fat and had gone on a diet and stayed on it.

The wind, with nowhere specific to go, brought her to her tippy-toes, and me too, not Mammy though; she was my anchor, she was heavy, she knew what it took to stay on her feet. A gust of wind made the old woman wobble on the pavement and then she fell in front of an artic and it burst her open – it was like watching a balloon burst. Her blood landed on my face and in my eyes and on my mouth. I stood there. I don't remember the brakes squealing and they have must have done, because I would turn rigid from thereon in any time I heard even the mildest squeal. Nor do I remember the blood spatter on my mother's face and coat, and it must have been there. I remember staring at my hand … it was held out, as if I was about to catch something.

Benny's mother, she was. And she wasn't as old as I thought she'd been. She'd been built like a sapling. People kept saying I was lucky – it could have been me that the wind took. They said that to Mammy – the shopkeeper said it to her too as he gave Mammy all she wanted. And he gave me Trigger bars, saying I could have a cola if I'd stop crying. I simply had to stop crying. But I couldn't do that for ages and ages. I had cried before, of course, but the crying this time.…Well, it hurt to cry.

Through the mist in my eyes, I saw that I was in the shopkeeper's poky office. There were papers spread all over his desk and the walls had paintings of racehorses, politicians and old football teams. Every one of them, if not hung crooked to begin with, ended up that way from people's shoulders brushing against them, or from doors that were closed too hard, which created breezes to knock them off kilter. A wind had roared into my life and run me through like a sword. It had left everything in its wake disturbed.

2

Of late, caused by the rough shaking down of his health last year, his long-dead first wife is once more substantial in his mind. He sees her as she was, before life set to poisoning her. People here in this sleepy little Pennsylvania town know nothing of the circumstances surrounding her murder – Cheston Lower is a place that keeps its nose to itself. And those in the town where she was killed, back in Ireland, have probably forgotten about her.

This fine sunny September morning, Dan Somers is sitting out on his back veranda, after putting the PVC hood on the barbeque. The end of the garden runs into forest and occasionally a deer wanders from it and comes right up to the edge of the decking. There are squirrels, pine martens, rats, wild cats and bears. A neighbour, Red Berry, told him once about a neighbour and her encounter with a mountain lion. 'It came and ate Holly Darling up, when was it, sixty-nine, could have been seventy. Wasn't much of her left anyways – the State Troopers shot her, the cat, but I think they plugged Holly too – she was breathing, see, just about, that's all. Scared the dandy out of us, all that bad wheezing … but that's it … just so you know that you and your missus there should never leave the back door open. House was a mess, I remember, though they painted the place up, the couple who bought it, they was still finding specks of Holly's blood here and there a year later.'

Dan had bought the house cheap. He hasn't mentioned Holly's tale to Irene, because she has a hang-up about living in a house where someone died. He'd asked Red to keep his lips zipped about it too. But if she was half the psychic she claimed to be, she shouldn't have to be told zing. *Where is she?* Last-minute packing. Deciding which pack of mumbo jumbo cards to bring along. She reads the tarot, says she's a confidant of spirits. Malarkey. He'd let her read his cards, just to humour her, but she saw the humouring and got thick as a heavy snowfall, cancelled the read – took her ages to thaw too. Flare-ups … always damn serious when they happen.

The thing is, they know they can live without each other, and sometimes the fact is a comfort they both draw upon, for no reason other than it is a comfort.

He is going home, to Ireland. Home? How you can call it that, Irene had asked after he'd mooted the idea a while back, when he had gotten back on his feet. Home is where the heart is, she said, into his silence.

It's not that he wants to go – it is more, he thinks, to do with being lured. There is money waiting for him, and documents awaiting his signature. Also, there is an end he wants to put to some things.

In his dreams, she is forever smiling … laughing, her voice soft and quiet. He used to ask himself how such a gentle voice could wound so deeply. Yet there was something to her, a vulnerability, a store of hidden kindnesses and dreams abandoned.

He closes his eyes. Brings his old town to mind. Contrasting smells in the early morning. Freshly baked bread from the bakery in the town square and of death from the abattoir a mile downhill, to the east. You cannot remember one without remembering the other. That old eastern wind used to carry the smell of burning offal into the town, for it to mingle with the smell wafting from the bakery's ovens. Good and bad. Evil is not in the trench opposite you, he thinks, as in World War I, but instead it's in your own, in that vein dug into the earth, and you can't always see evil for what it is.

He hears the fly screen open, slam home, the subtle creaks in the deck boards.

'Hon?' Irene says.

He opens his eyes.

'Breakfast. You should eat something before the taxi arrives,' she says.

'Okay, thanks.'

'Are you all right?'

'Yeah, fine.'

She puts the polka-dotted tray on the round table, next to yesterday's *Cheston Herald*. 'Thanks,' he says, putting the newspaper on his lap to guard against orange juice and coffee spillage. He's wearing tan chinos and unlike his usual navy denims, they don't hide piss drops – so the newspaper is a habit thing.

Thirty-one years is a long time to be away from a place, a person, even a dead one. Only days into his fifty-second year, he had not expected to find himself in this position, travelling to a place he calls home but which isn't and hasn't been for a long time; the people as his people. But cancer shakes the living shit out of you and gives your heart a telescopic eye to look at your mortality, the world at large – it relaxes you a little, calms the soul, maybe. You can, with the eye of a sniper, hit the mark when it comes to distinguishing between what is and isn't important. Sometimes you forget the brush with death, but reminders are never too distant.

The last time he was in Heuston Station, a man with drink singing on his lips told him how he had acquired his prosthetic leg. His name was Joey and he had been a corporal in the British army. While on foot patrol in Northern Ireland, he'd kicked at a booby-trapped door. He was on his way to Galway to visit a former military colleague. He spoke of breaking it off with his girlfriend because he could do nothing for her. Telling Dan, in other words, that the explosion had taken away more than just his leg. When he asked why Dan had tears in his eyes, the reply arrived quietly yet brutally. The former soldier averted his gaze and coughed to clear his throat, perhaps of wayward tears.

Now he is here. In Heuston, after many years. The trains are more modern. The station is no longer the drab, cold terminal of Dan's youth. Still, there are pigeons, more brazen than their ancestors in their quest for crumbs. Though perhaps he is mistaken. Memories are fluid and generally not cast in stone.

His travelling companion is his second wife. Irene. She keeps her maiden name, Gaston. She used be an ultra-feminist, but the years have chipped away at her stance and now she's against injustices in general and not just those perpetrated against women. Dan is not sure if this is progress.

She sits on the bench, eyeing up the coffee kiosk and wondering if she should get a refill, along with the free sample of Butler's chocolate. She's weighing the idea against his reminding her that she has Type 2 diabetes. That's if the coffee and chocolate would be worth having, after listening to his reminder. Such a skinny woman, she couldn't believe her doctor's diagnosis. In her ignorance, she'd believed only fat people were prone to catching the disease.

This is her first time in Ireland, in Europe. It's too soon for her to tell Dan what she thinks about the Emerald Isle – she'll look, listen, ponder on all of her observations and then hit him between the eyes with the good and the bad, in her own kind and usual way.

'What are you thinking about, hon?' she says.

He tells her about Joey the one-legged soldier.

'That's sad,' she says.

'It is.'

'Maybe you can look him up,' she says.

Daft notion, he thinks.

'Why would I do that? He wasn't a friend, just someone I met and talked with for half an hour.'

He acts quickly to cut her off by saying that he knows what she's loaded onto the tip of her tongue: that Joey and he must have known each other in a previous life. Irene and her tarot. His inner jury is out on that sort of stuff; there are times when he is firmly convinced there is nothing to it, and other moments when his views are less than entrenched. Someone once told him that she was very good. He has never asked anyone to define what exactly 'very good' means. Though one day, after he'd worked on the bag at the gym – reliving his juvenile years when he'd boxed – he was in to collect a Thai takeaway Irene had ordered when a black woman tapped him on the shoulder and said, 'You Irene's husband, still?'

'I am,' he smiled. *Still.* He felt good after the workout, light in himself. Young.

'I was thinking you was – I saw you in the garden as I was calling in to her for a reading, maybe a year ago – she said I was going to have a baby and every doctor, every baby doctor I had gone to had said no way was that going to happen for me. You tell her from me that I have a baby boy that I delivered myself to the world. You tell her Floress said that.'

He wanted to say that she should tell Irene herself, and wondered why she hadn't. Perhaps for the same reason people don't do such things: they always intend to, but life just gets in the way until they eventually forget.

A train draws home with a tiny screech.

'I'm going to have another coffee,' she says, 'and don't you go harping on about my sugar levels, eh? Let me enjoy my treat.'

He watches as she strolls to the kiosk and then turns his eyes to the breaking news on the large TV screen. Some famous young footballer dead from a heart attack on the pitch. He was as young as Dan had been, the last time he sat here. Alone, shivering, not a coin in his pocket.

Not an hour after, a doctor had approached him in a hospital corridor and said there was nothing he could do to save his wife. He remembers Joey, remembers his slow nodding, his squeeze on his upper arm, the sudden thirst that seized the former paratrooper and led him away to the bar. The bad limp, swaying on his dummy leg – perhaps not yet practiced enough – hands in his coat pockets. A swapping of stories under the high roof of a train station terminal and the pain ringing loudly in their hearts, pain nothing either of them could salve, for that was Time's duty alone.

Irene offers him half of her chocolate bar and he takes it, lets it melt in his mouth, squeezes the red wrapper small and stands.

'You going somewhere, hon?'

'Restroom.'

'You just went.'

'Drink your coffee.'

He puts the wrapper in the waste bin. He can feel her eyes on his back as he crosses the esplanade to the restrooms. In his younger days, he called them toilets. Restroom is a better choice … it is where waste comes to rest, he supposes.

Her eyes fall to his fly as he rejoins her. She is a woman who misses nothing, though she sometimes pretends that she does. She worries about his prostate more than he does – but he occasionally thinks that she carries many of his worries for him.

'You okay?' she says.

'Yeah, you?'

He takes her hand and squeezes. She smiles. He loves her big brown eyes, the way her soul seems to light them up.

Does she know I'm hiding stuff from her?

A draught blows in from the north, pours in through the large doors as they slide back and forth, coming off the rippled back of the river – there are hooks in that draught, capable of spearing fish.

There are more foreigners here, Middle Eastern, African, than there were in 1983. He could tell that at a glance from looking out of the bus they'd rode into the station. The world is getting smaller and smaller – what brought them here is what sent many Irish to the States. He went too, but for reasons that weren't purely economic.

It's late. They'd delayed in the city centre to beat the commuter rush hour. On the train, they sit in seats nearest the loo and the baggage area. The evening light is beginning to fade. A whistle blows and an announcement in the carriage says that the train is about to depart.

Irene points when she sees a pair of brown donkeys in a field, one chawing on the other's neck. When they cross the canal at Robertstown, at a barge beginning a turn, she draws his attention to it, disturbing his thoughts, disrupting the images in his mind, freezing the scenes. He has learned to be patient when she talks too much, when she annoys him – she is a natural talker, but now and then, she talks just to lead him from dark places.

Darkness shrouds the windows, hides the landscape but not the apparitions of their faces.

Irene is taken by the announcements of the stations they stop at – given in Irish and then in English. She likes the orange neon bricks in the rectangular signs that relay information in both languages. Cute, she says, meaning strange, interesting and new.

'Can you speak Irish?' she says, touching him in the side. He has the window seat.

'No.'

'Why not?'

He shrugs. Do I tell her I hated the frigging way teachers rammed it down our throats, about the corporal punishment they meted out? He decides against.

'I just didn't.'

'I see – do many people speak it?'

'Irene,' he says, 'I have no idea – I've been out of the country for decades – I don't know this country anymore – I don't think that I ever did to begin with.'

'Must be stirring up a lot of memories for you then, this journey?'

Obviously, he thinks.

'This is why I suggested that you stay at home – I'm not sure if I'm going to be good company.'

A laugh. 'Oh, hon, you're far from that at the best of times.'

He studies his reflection in the darkened window and turns to her, allowing a smile to flourish for moments.

'Are you thinking about this meeting with your sister?' she says.

'No. I haven't lent it much thought, not yet.'

A blatant fib. He does not want to discuss his sister. He hadn't spoken to her much in all the time he'd been in the States, until about six weeks ago when she got word to him about the house. She'd contacted his old workplace and they forwarded the letter on to August Antiques. He finds the job less pressurised than dealing with public money. He gets to see some interesting stuff and likes the bargaining aspect. There are times it's as much as he can do to keep himself within his own skin – nerve trouble, drifting clouds of anxiety attacks. Nighttimes are worse. Irene thinks it might be the past, a thing deep-rooted, a stone working its way to the surface, the way stones do. Sometimes it is the past, but lately it's fear. A fear of the future, of dying. An acute awareness which too frequently grips him, vice-like, that death's sting will one day touch him. Consoles himself, whenever he focuses on people who are dead – *at least it is behind her, done with.* A curious concept of which to be envious, he thinks.

'I'm sure everything will be all right … wait and see,' Irene says.

He had wanted to put the past behind him, to push it far away, for sea fog to shroud it. There were times when the fog cleared, and he felt in slow time the layers of the years peel one by one from his essence. She had not deserved to die in such a brutal fashion – whoever killed her had gotten away clean. Often the fact stuck in his throat like a fish bone. Now he was being drawn back to Ireland, to deal with a sister and a brother-in-law intent on cheating him out of money due to him – he wondered if this was a nudge from beyond, before his health completely failed him, a prompt for him to search for answers.

It was a matter he should have dealt with years ago. Searched for truth, shaken every branch of every tree in pursuit of it. And there were moments when he had steeled himself to do just that, but his resolve never acquired motion: he would allow a work matter or some other distraction to take over, and the momentum was lost, and the fog would steal in. In addition, he would argue with himself that he owed Ena nothing; he had spent enough time on her, loving her. His mother's words were haunting echoes – she was common, with no breeding, and would let him down. But he had loved her, oh so much, and believed she loved him – believed that if left alone they could fix the other's faults, because they were good together. Or if not good, then less broken than when they were apart. Irene? Should he tell her about Ena? Of his real intentions for returning to Ireland? To solve the money matter, but also to delve into Ena's murder? To see a cop, a name he remembered from the past, who he had rung looking for at the Garda station in Kildarragh, a man who'd called him back, who remembered the case, who said he would help in any way he could, though he expressed doubt that any progress would be made.

It might destroy their relationship, if he divulges the truth. She knows only a little of his past and he of hers. Relationships are, he supposes, a bit like joining the Foreign Legion – you lose your past identity in order to survive. She will pull a freaker if he reveals it – she wants to visit the land of the druids, get to see a leprechaun, visit the homeland of her ancestors. A mention of Ena and her unsolved murder, that he was a prime suspect, would ruin things. Their relationship had hit choppy waters until he'd fallen ill. It had become a tired relationship given fresh impetus by adversity.

He has reason to visit Ireland. While he is back he has to avail of the opportunity to ask around, knock on doors, see if an answer had ever turned up, a deathbed confession – many of those who knew him would now be off the life stage, but others would not, might still be around, might be holding a secret close, but maybe not so tightly anymore – the shock of seeing him might dislodge it – he could see enough in an instant to encourage him to pry further.

3

Because he does not talk to her, because she had asked him several questions he had not answered, her thoughts shifted to her family. The sisters she likes, those she doesn't. A brother she can't stand, in-laws she calls out-laws, a stepmother she would happily do time in a state penitentiary for killing – a mother for whom she would willingly endure a lethal injection if she could find her to kill. Words fail her when it comes to her former mother-in-law.

'Are we here?' she says, the train slowing.

'Last stop,' he replies.

'Oh, great, you found your tongue,' she says.

He gives her a neutral look.

She looks at her watch, slips on her red Parka and checks her handbag to see she has everything. He hauls their luggage from the rack area onto the aisle. Since she lost her passport and her purse in Mexico four years ago, she triple-checks. Whenever she's tired, she forgets she's checked and re-checks minutes later. Forgetfulness, she says, is a symptom of diabetes. She would hate to contract Alzheimer's. 'God, spare me that pot of shit of yours,' she often says. A friend of theirs has it. Thirty-six years old and there are moments when she can't remember the names of the children she gave birth to.

4

He sometimes takes consolation from the fact that that Irene and he never had a child – they will never have to witness one suffer. Maybe it's not a good way of looking at things, and his guess is that it's not entirely healthy, but it helps him to ward off the angst that visits whenever he thinks he would have loved to have had a son, a daughter, in his life. It is beginning to sit badly with him that there are things he has not discussed with Irene. Things concerning his past, his late wife – she knows he was married before and that the marriage failed to work out. That her name was Ena. Apart from this, she knows precious little else.

He had seen in Irene, he thought, not so much a physical likeness to Ena – there was a little, in the angle of her jawline and in her thinness – but something else more prominent that he'd learned from listening to her, and these were inner scars in a slow process of healing. Not to be probed too deeply though, as his own weren't, not if they wanted a clear road ahead of them – he knows now that the past likes to plant landmines along the road called the future.

Like Ena, he suspected, she had a rough upbringing. He was sometimes given to wondering what had shaped her. These days he understood what had patterned Ena's life – her family, the poverty, and, he suspected, sexual abuse. He was too young and naive back then to consider these issues

– he had been blind to everything, except his love for her. She drank to numb herself against the pain – it became her crutch. She would, he now believed, have done anything to stop the past from coming to visit her. He saw this trait in Irene, albeit in a different way – she'd turned to reading the tarot and believed herself to be a psychic. A better route to take than drink, he was certain. But in actual fact, she'd saved herself by getting the hell out of her home place. Ena had left it too late to get out of hers. He had felt the same thing for Irene that he'd felt for Ena – a protective instinct to save them.

He sees Ena now, in his mind's eye, on the platform. She looks beautiful.

'Here,' Irene says, offering him the handle of his stroller case, her's already extended.

They feed tickets into the automated stiles and pass through, out and under the archway into the cold Kildarragh air. From where he is standing, he can smell nothing.

5

It's fall and blooming freezing outside the station. Where they live, at this time of year, she thinks, they could sit out on the veranda and not feel the pinch of a breeze. There isn't a cab in sight, just a broad spread of empty parking lot. Across the road, chimney pots are exhaling greyish smoke against the starry night.

Seems a quiet town. The air freshened by a recent shower of rain. He is silent. He doesn't think to tell her things and she often refrains from allowing her tongue to walk in on his thoughts.

'Is it too far to walk into town?' she asks. 'Maybe we should catch a cab, eh?'

Dan is standing there as if he doesn't know what to do next. Like a thousand ghosts are waiting in line to shake his hand.

'Dan,' she says, a little louder.

He looks at her. 'I think we should walk, Skinny.'

'Skinny' is what he sometimes calls her. He says it in a nice way, though she wonders if she was fat, would he call her 'Fatso'. She's not sure if it's possible for that word to be said with fondness.

He'd booked a room online in The Prince Harold, called after some medieval earl who liked to wear flashy clothes. The B&B adjoins a fifteenth-century keep that looks kind of spooky and derelict. As he was surfing the net he beckoned her over to show off a sequence of photographs. She pretended to be impressed; she thinks it's often best to be like that with someone who's trying their hardest to please and believes their effort is good enough.

It's a constant battle to keep him from going into a mood. She does it because she feels for him, has done since the first moment she clapped eyes on him in the consignment store where she worked for a while. She had a natural eye for appraising the quality of antiques. Afterwards, he always came to her for advice, and soon afterwards, he asked her out to dinner. They found each other easy company. She knows well what it's like when a man and a woman constantly jar against each other, having suffered that experience with her first husband, Louis. She'd sensed that he was doing the dirt on her and when she put her suspicions to him, he broke down and swore he was sorry, begged her not to leave him. He asked who had told her about the affair and she said no one. She knew. She packed and walked and swore to God Almighty that she would have nothing to do with another man for as long as breath passed through her. Men were where a woman's dream went to die.

They set off on the footpath. She's thankful that the breeze is behind them. The way is uphill mostly, a gradual climb. Dan doesn't say much beyond them not having much further to walk. He points to the cathedral on the small hill, the thousand-year-old round tower in its grounds, which to her resembles a giant penis. King Kong Knob. She doesn't say that to him, as he could be in his reverent mood. He's an occasional God man, which is worse, she thinks, than being someone who is a God man 24/7. You know where you stand with the latter.

They stop off in the pub, which is part of the B&B, and check in. They order food and then the barman shows them across to their room. It's okay, basic. But she makes out to Dan it's the Taj Mahal.

'Really?' he says.

'No, not anywhere near really.'

'It's only for a couple of nights.'

'The bed is bouncy enough,' she says, sitting on it.

'The room is cold – but the radiator is piping,' he says.

She lies on the bed and kicks off her shoes. It's good to take your weight off the world for a while. He's in the restroom now, flushing the toilet. He does that wherever they book into a place, flushes when there's no need. The extractor fan comes on. She wouldn't mind sleeping for a while, and waking up in about an hour to try it on with him, which she often likes to do. But he might not want to, seeing as they're in memory territory, which could well be hostile. Besides, she thinks, their food is on the way back in the pub, so that hangs that idea by its tail.

He has only told her a little about Ena. She has only told him a little about Louis. A little sounded even too much for them to tell and to hear. The past is a foreign country, some writer wrote, but it's never as foreign as she would like – the past can land on your lap and choke up your present, and your future.

The pub is pleasant. They find a space to themselves in the tiniest nook and eat fries and cheeseburgers. Photographs of the local drama group are on the walls – a small trophy cabinet holds programmes, newspaper cuttings of various successes on the drama festival circuit. 'The Prince Harry Players,' blares one headline, 'Do Athlone and Win the All Ireland Drama Festival.'

She once had a walk-on part in *Friends*, as a waitress bringing coffee to a table. A friend got her the role, such as it was. A fleeting second of fame – she wouldn't recognise herself if she saw the clip run across the TV. She was much skinnier now– skinny pretty and not skinny haggard – and her hair was a lot longer and a different colour. It is presently black and short, but she is considering getting in a reddish colour. Her name didn't even feature on the credits. And the coffee wasn't even real, for crying out loud. It kind of ruined for her the whole mystique of TV and the movies. Watching TV, she can no longer totally immerse herself in the surrealism, as she's too vividly aware of the cameras looking in on the set, the way the actors walk away after playing their part, stepping back into their real selves. Just like that, it seemed. She thinks very many actors are bound to suffer from a crisis of identity. Must do, when you consider the diversity of characters they take on throughout their careers.

'Guinness,' Dan says to her.

Not a question.

She'd promised to sample it. She fails to understand how anyone can bring their lips, let alone their stomach, to that black sludge. He used to keep a few cans of the stuff in the fridge and then he started on Irish whiskey, and because she could drink that with him, he left off with the tar slick, so he hasn't had a pint of Guinness in years. He says.

'Half a pint then,' he says, showing mercy.

'Okay, Dan. What's half a pint? A midget glass?'

He shows her the measure with his hands and she nods.

She watches the guy at the pump. He's Polish or maybe Latvian. She would have liked an Irish barman to serve them. It feels like the time she went to an Amish heritage park in Pennsylvania and they were selling these cute little mementoes, and she turned them over to learn with horror that they'd been made in China. 'What the heck?' she'd said to herself. It surely has to be a huge disappointment to Chinese tourists when they visit the States, in the sense that a holiday is meant to take you away from home. Dan thinks differently – he said the Chinese Amish community in Hong Kong manufactured the knick-knacks. The Ghanaians brewed Guinness, he added, and that didn't make it lose any of its Irishness. He's probably right, though she doesn't think there are Amish in China.

The barman sits the pint and half pint on a green drip tray on the counter, waiting for them to settle before he tops them up with the milky part. Scum on swamp juice.

'Well?' he says, after she takes her first taste of black beer.

'It wouldn't be high on my list of preferences.'

He takes a mighty quaff to say he's in major disagreement.

'We'll go,' he says, 'unless you want to stay on a while?'

'No, I'm bushed.'

Outside, it's bitterly cold. The keep doesn't wear any lights, its small windows blind. Dan mentions that a baby's spirit haunts the keep and cries on specific nights at specific times.

'That's why it's no longer occupied, I guess,' he says, turning the key in the main door to the B&B area.

'Yeah,' she says, 'but I'd say that has more to do with it being cold and damp and plain spooky looking. Doesn't follow that it has a ghosty baby.'

Room number 5. They're both wrecked and the earlier friskiness in her has worn away.

She undresses in the bathroom and looks herself over. She can't believe she is the person in the mirror. Wrinkles trail along her forehead like abandoned railway tracks, and a trench platoon from WWI would gladly commandeer the lines about her eyes. What is she going to look like in twenty years? Inner quakes cause the skin to fracture, as much as time does, she reckons. Is it better to be dead than old? Time is definitely the devil's torture chamber.

In bed, she waits for Dan to emerge from the john. She doesn't want to settle in for sleep before kissing and hugging him goodnight first. She hears him fart and belch, stuff he never does at home. She blames the Guinness, though it could be the horsemeat acting up. He doesn't know it was horsemeat – most people can't tell the difference – she can. She doesn't mind eating horsemeat. And she knows her beef, too, having eaten all sorts, being hungry enough in her younger days to lose fussiness when it came to food.

'DAN!' she calls when he lets rip a humdinger.

He comes out, the toilet flushing in his wake.

'Okay, okay, okay,' he says, turning around. 'I forgot.'

Irene has a rule – if you leave the bathroom with the toilet still flushing, you haven't spent nearly enough time washing your hands.

He eases into bed beside her, bringing his side down. He could do with losing some weight. His belly always squishes against her whenever they're making love – it's like there's a waterbed draped over her. If she mentions his weight, he sulks. It's not that he's obese: he is overweight and she is thin. She is sure he feels her bones prod at his flesh, but it doesn't bother him enough to lay off his food and beer for a bit. Since his illness, he has piled on the weight.

Before his scare, he'd kept it in check by hitting the punch bag a couple of evenings a week, and there was a hint in his gait that suggested he could handle himself. Now, he looked like it pained him to breathe.

They turn off bedside lamps and hug for a few seconds before turning their backs to each other to sleep.

In the silence, the dark and long silence, she feels the sleepiness abandon her, and she thinks, 'Ah here....'

She faces into Dan's back, but he's already lightly snoring. She pokes him a little and says, 'If you're up for it, big boy.'

He snores. And she pokes him harder, this time to stop him snoring.

She edges into sleepiness, grateful for its arrival.

And dreams of a baby crying.

6

He wakes to hear Irene in the shower. Hears the water pouring. He needs the loo. His sister, Teresa, is meeting them in the pub at midday, to talk about the house, give him a key to have a final look around the old family home. Frosty women, Teresa and Irene, in different ways. Older than him by five years, Teresa married a local racehorse trainer. They emigrated to New Zealand after Revenue fined them for cooking their accounting books. They both have extravagant tastes, and like many people who do, they turn obnoxious when challenged on their indulgences.

'Dan,' Irene says, tiptoeing naked to the bed where she'd laid out her clothes, 'do you think my grey cords and moccasins are okay?'

'Yeah.'

'The lemon polo?'

'Sure.'

'You don't think it's too gimpy looking?'

He has no idea what that word means. She always uses it, and once when he'd asked her what it meant, she shrugged and said, 'You know, don't be silly.'

'It's not gimpy,' he says.

'Hmm.'

She dresses.

*

Teresa has gained weight. She's waiting, along with her husband Billy J., whom Dan doesn't like very much. Or hadn't, when he knew him. After introductions, they sit around a table in the lounge area of the pub. They order cappuccinos and these arrive with little cellophane-wrapped biscuits on the saucer. Irene is all talk, building bridges over the lapses into awkwardness. Billy J. puts his white cloth cap beside him, between Teresa and him. Dan gets the notion there is more than just the cap dividing the couple.

Billy J., he remembers, had stout bandy legs, as if he was a human horseshoe, and walking always appeared an effort for him. Always stocky, the weight is now hanging off his face, giving him a hound-dog expression. Dark circles under his eyes suggest to Dan a pattern of lost sleep, constant pain, or the spear points of guilt.

Billy J. and Teresa are trying to screw him; after he stymies their plan, they will rely on family blood for clemency. He isn't sure if he wants to give it – but his father comes to mind and he can't help feeling he would like him to let things go. His father was like that, easy-going, the total opposite to his mother. Yet, even for her, he might go along with the idea of letting the couple off the hook. He used to be so angry with his mother, but she'd gotten it right about Ena, as much as it sickened his gut to admit. And the antagonism between them over Ena, well … it must have played a part, no matter how small, in his mother's heart attack.

'That's a lovely outfit, Teresa,' Irene says.

Her glance tells him that Teresa does not shop in a consignment store. He remembers their mother chiding Teresa for spending too much money on clothes, her wedding, herself in general.

'320,000 euros,' Teresa says, killing the small talk, producing documentation for him to look at.

The cheque made out to Dan is for a little less than half the sale amount. She mentions deductions for this and that fee. Hands him the invoices. A large display to show that she has been honourable in her dealings, which Dan knows is not true.

'A good price,' Teresa says, as he looks at the fees charged.

He nods. They'd barely spoken since he left Ireland. Most of his letters and emails to her went unanswered. He'd called the solicitor because with Teresa, sometimes you can read the turns she's going to take. Billy J. claps his hand lightly on his thigh, as though to stamp a deal.

'The house has been let since I moved out, Teresa,' Dan says.

Her lips pucker and her cheeks and throat flush. Billy J. looks away, sits his cap on his thigh.

'That's thirty years' half-rent you owe me,' Dan says.

Teresa wrings her hands. There is a clash from the gold bands on her fingers, a miniature brake squeal.

Irene says, 'Teresa, why didn't you answer Dan's letters and emails? For the years I've been with Dan, you kept silent as a dead mouse. You ignored him right up until you wanted to sell the house.'

'Truth is, we're skint,' Billy J. says, looking at the lining in his cap.

'That's not Dan's problem – years of half rent is a hell of a lot of money,' Irene says. 'You guys need to reconfigure that cheque.'

'Say 1,500 for each year,' Dan says, 'so 30,000. I think that's fair. I'm only factoring in twenty years' worth of rent.'

Billy J., he thinks, is primed to take a turn. Teresa chews on her upper lip.

She says weakly, after a tight cough, 'Okay.'

They both watch as Teresa scribbles another cheque and hands it over – the cheque resembles a fluttering wing between her thumb and forefinger.

Billy J. coughs and says, 'You need to sign those documents for the solicitor, to show that everything's above board.'

'I will, after the cheques clear,' Dan says.

He knows the cheques will bounce higher than a basketball dropped from the balcony of a sixth-floor apartment.

Irene says, 'I think that's a reasonable proposition. I'm quite sure you understand.'

Teresa shoots Irene a hard look, as though asking who the hell is she to open her mouth on the matter.

'We're leaving tomorrow,' Billy J. says with something close to panic.

'Tomorrow?' Irene says.

Teresa says, 'I told the solicitor I'd have the papers with him by this afternoon.'

Dan shakes his head. 'It's not going to happen.'

Irene, sharp as, after refocusing, says, 'We're here for ten more days – we can give the papers to the solicitor after the money clears.'

Silence.

'Maybe we should all go and visit the solicitor,' Irene suggests. 'I can't see the sense in discussing this matter here – quite frankly, it sucks … I dunno….'

Billy J.'s mild blue eyes moisten. His ample tummy strains his shirt buttons. He holds out his fat clammy hands, shakes his head. It's as though he's found himself burgled of words.

Teresa moves her lips to one side and then the other, as though she's chewing on something.

'I've already spoken to him,' Dan says sternly, 'the day before yesterday.'

This is news to Irene, though she tries to show it isn't. Should have told her, he thinks.

'Teresa,' Dan says, 'I want you to be honest with me for the next five minutes and then you can go back to being the way you are normally.'

'Hon,' Irene says, touching the small silver cross hanging from her neck.

He gives her the look he uses to switch her to silence – to let her know he'll be with her in a minute, that he's busy at present. Can she not see? Not a hard look, just advisory, but the shortest of steps from being a glare.

'Nothing,' she says, thinking it's high time she pulled him up.

Billy J. says, 'Look–'

Dan cuts in, dismissing him with a slight wave. 'Teresa?'

'No,' Billy J. sallies back. 'Listen. Your mother willed the house to Teresa and you – whichever of you didn't already own a house could live there – with the money to be split from the sale of the house if it were to be sold.'

'I know that.'

'What Billy J. is saying is this,' Teresa says. 'We don't own a house – we could decide to live there and you'd get nothing. Zero.'

'Well, why don't you guys move into it?' Irene says.

'Never,' Billy J. says. 'We're well settled where we are. Back to wind and rain? No thanks.'

'Well you need to figure something out. You owe a lot of people a lot of money,' Dan counters abruptly.

'We need this break, I won't lie,' Teresa admits. The fight has fled from her tone.

'Your cheques – they'll bounce,' he says, 'yeah?'

33

Irene says, 'Hon, how do you know that?'

He goes on, 'Teresa?'

She nods.

'I rang and warned the solicitor right from the off about your previous history, so he knew you were a dubious pair.'

'My god – you should both be swung by the neck from the nearest tree,' Irene says, adding, 'sister, my foot – I know your kind – I have one just like you.'

A song Irene used to like, 'Alone Again, Naturally' begins to play. Of a sudden she is at a pokey barn at a local hop, and a boy called Harris Jones is trying to lean his hard on against her.

'How do we fix this?' Irene says, reeling herself into the present.

'The deal is on hold,' Dan says.

'What?' Teresa says.

Billy J. says, 'You're not serious? Jesus….'

'I am very serious.'

Teresa says, 'But the buyer—"

'Disappointed, but that's life.'

'So,' Billy J. says, 'we're going back to renting it, is that the game plan?'

Dan understands that Billy J. is clutching at any straw of income, for a little is better than none.

'No,' Dan says.

'No?' Teresa says, reeling.

'Hon,' Irene says, touching his elbow, 'you let her go on for a long, long time, why did you allow that to happen?'

'I don't know,' Dan says, eyes on Teresa. 'I was managing okay, I guess – she used to be my sister.'

7

My, Irene thinks, you can live with a person for five years and all of a sudden you're looking at him, thinking, who is this man? It's a bit like catching sight of the far side of the moon.

She says this to him in the late afternoon in the café at the Japanese Gardens. She'd just bought a T-shirt in the tourist office for their old neighbour, Red Berry. She knew he'd be delighted by the logo: 'Irish National Stud'.

She brings it for a peep out of the bag. Dan says Red won't like the colour, maybe she should exchange it for a red to go with his name and get a small size as the medium will hang off him.

'What's eating you?' she says.

He remains silent, like a flipping roadkill. She sits silently too.

She likes the gardens, the many and varied scents of the shrubs and flowers. According to the brochure, the Japanese Gardens map out man's journey through life. Adjoining the gardens is the stud: horses, the stallion boxes, barns and paddocks. But looking at these had bored her. The skeleton of a famous horse in the museum hadn't impressed her either. Dead bones are meant to rest in the clay and aren't for gawking at. Like the bog bodies she'd googled in the Irish Museum and that skeleton of a Viking warrior. People

don't know when to let things rest. Or they do, but won't
let them. Dan is sitting with his legs crossed. He's wearing
a straw hat like her grandfather wore. There are so many
tourists here. Japanese visiting a Japanese Garden – why, she
thinks.

The smoke from his cigarette swirls in front of his face
like a cloud of thin fog. He disperses it with a couple of flaps
of his hand.

She cuts the fruit scone and butters both halves. Spreads
jam on his and not on hers.

'Your scone, with jam, just the way you like it,' she says.

He pinches his nose, raises his sunglasses above his eyes.
She is lost as to why the hell he's wearing those. There's no
sun.

'Aren't you going to tell me,' she says, 'what you should
have told me back home?'

He shifts on his bum, as if the question has stung. He
looks off, eyes on the pretty Japanese woman trailing her
group. There are moments when she forgets what it is that
she sees in him. Thinks on when they first met. He'd said
he was fascinated by the way she spoke, the accent. How
she said 'awf' instead of 'off', or 'I'm fixing to go here …'
and other remnants of her southern-style lingo. She'd left
North Carolina when she was five and began to learn a new
tongue, just so she wouldn't sound out of place in her New
Jersey school. Kids still taunted, though, and used to get her
to say words they considered a howl.

'I'm waiting, hon, what's gotten into you?'

'Nothing,' he says.

A bee hovers above his scone. He waves it away. Picks a
raisin and eats it, then he starts on the scone.

'Why didn't you tell me about your grand scheme, Dan?'

'What are you talking about?'

'This house business.'

'Didn't I tell you?'

'You most certainly did not.'

'Lower your voice,' he says, reaching for a paper napkin.

She spits words through her teeth. 'You level with me, buster, or I'm out of here, right now, right home, this frigging afternoon.'

'Okay, okay,' he says, resting his elbows on the table, 'there's something that I need to do, and I should have said this to you sooner, yes, I know. But....'

'But?'

'I never told you the full story about Ena.'

His eyes lock on hers. There is, she thinks, a weight in his look.

'I want to check up on a few things about her. I need to sort out something.'

'We're supposed to be on holiday. The deal was for you to visit her grave, and then to carry on with the break, right?'

'This is why I couldn't keep you up to speed. I knew you'd give me your attitude.'

'Attitude. Frigging attitude?'

'I'm ... let's not row.'

'Stop squirming your way, hon, and just say the hell what's on your mind.'

He coughs and begins. 'Ena–'

'What did she look like?'

He draws a deep breath into him and slowly exhales, his eyes filling.

'I want to know,' Irene says.

'She had red hair, pale complexion, and almond-shaped eyes. Green. She was a year older than me and worked in a pharmacy and before that in a fast food joint.'

He pauses for breath.

When it looks like he's not going to continue, she prompts him. He's staring at some spot on the floor, eyes fixed there. 'We dated for a year, got married, honeymooned down south, and rented an apartment down a little laneway by the cathedral. Firecastle Lane. It was a grubby little place. A lightbulb always had to be on if you wanted any light – it was dark, dank and damp and constantly smelled of something like cabbage cooking.'

'A big change of accommodation for you, more so than for her,' Irene says, with an edge that draws his eyes to hers.

She sees the strain in his face, the giveaway small tremors in his cheeks and chin.

He says, 'It wasn't too long before we started rowing. It was over money usually – what else? And her smoking and drinking habits. Then it grew into rowing over other things apart from money. Petty arguments sprang wild, onto a larger canvas.'

He pauses.

'I see,' Irene says into the silence.

'Pretty soon,' he says, 'she started staying out late and I would go searching for her in the pubs – we had twenty-two pubs in the town and two hotels – it got messy. It all got very messy....'

Words jam in his throat and he throws his hands to the air, like he has given up hope for Ena once more.

Irene says, 'I'm sure I can figure out what sort of girl she was like – the loose sort who liked to drink more than her fair share and wasn't ever going to be shy with it came to fiddling about with men's mickeys.'

As soon as she finishes speaking, she detects a change in the atmosphere. His silence is deadly – he has shifted from being wounded and dwelling in self-pity to being consumed by a rising anger. She can all but see the smoke coming from him. She says to calm him, 'My younger sister, Chrissi, used that phrase to describe a loose woman. Chrissie is something else. Quiet as a corpse but then she'd up and come out with something to shock us all. Quiet people are ones to watch out for, for sure.'

Dan remains mute. He is no longer red-faced, but grey – grey, she believes, is the colour of true rage.

'When you caught up with her ...' she prompts.

Dan breathes heavily to clear his anger away and respond to her question. 'There'd be a massive row,' he says, 'it often got nasty when the man she was with turned on me. Worse than the meanest dog would do if you put your eyes to licking its bone. That sort of business went on for about six months.'

He is pressing the knuckles of his hand into the palm of the other. She hasn't seen him do that before.

He says, 'And don't ever speak ill of Ena again, Irene. You shouldn't speak ill of the dead.'

'Some people are dead while they're alive.'

'Just don't,' he says, his tone low with warning.

She feels as though he has just slapped her face. She goes to leave, says he's got a damn nerve speaking to her like that.

'Listen,' he says, his hand quickly seizing her wrist.

'Let go. People are watching.'

He releases his grip and says, 'Sorry. Listen ... please.'

She waits and stares at a woman at a table further down, until she looks away and minds her own business. 'One Saturday night there was an outdoor concert in the town's market square. She said she was staying over with a friend and I didn't answer her. I let her off and I went home – lit up a reefer and downed a few beers to forget about her. The first I knew of her going missing, as in really going missing, was a couple of days later, when her mother came pounding on the door, demanding money she said Ena owed her. I said I hadn't seen Ena in a couple of days and we both went to the guards – at her insistence – because, to tell you the truth, Ena had hurt me to a point beyond where I cared for her.'

'Really, Dan?' Irene says. 'It seems like you never stopped caring about her.'

He bites his lower lip, clearly struggling to keep a hold on his emotions. 'A tinker – a gypsy – he found her lying on the grasslands; she was splayed out in the bushes, across from a house she had left, after a party there.'

He rubs his hand over his thinning iron-grey hair, 'And they arrested me on suspicion of murdering her.' Irene nods. She realises now that everything comes out in the wash, eventually.

'I've heard enough for now,' Irene says. 'Enough,' she adds with steel.

8

He is waiting for her to speak and she has nothing to say. What he has just told her is swirling around inside her head.

He lights up a cigarette and stares out across the pond at the little Japanese filly crossing the bridge. She has a nice butt. Irene's caught him doing that sort of thing before – looking at young women whose skin would get the crawls if they knew.

He can read her like a book …. A murder suspect … my gawd. Did he…?

'Dan, that old feeling I used to get about you has come back to say hello. The impression that I am not your end line, that you are always on the lookout for someone better. What else haven't you told me?'

'You said enough for now.'

'I did … but you mean there's more?'

He nods.

'My God,' she says.

'Bear with me.'

His face is neutral, so she can't read it – is he for real?

'Bear with you,' she says, astounded. 'Do you know what this is doing to me … it's like a kick in the stomach. When you got the cancer, I knuckled down – I stayed. Do you forget we were nearly washed up? I stayed. I waited on you hand and foot, day and night. I worried day and night about you. I prayed the hardest I'd ever done, for you. I was there for you every goddamn inch of that journey, and you say bear with me. Who the hell are you, Dan? What sort of man lies to someone he's supposed to love? Who did so much for him?'

He doesn't respond.

'Do you know what?' she says, trying to keep her anxiety under control. 'I'm gonna walk around the gardens – I need to think a bit, okay?'

He doesn't try to stop her from leaving. In fact, he feels a little relieved to see her going; they need the space. Part of him wants to tell her that he loves her – the lying part of his heart. He knows she would not believe him, and also there would be no real meaning in it, for he would be saying it to merely steady their ship. It has all gone badly wrong and he had not meant for it to happen – he thinks to tell her this, but the opportunity is gone. Anything he says now would be far too little and much too late.

9

In the gardens she breathes in the smell of eucalyptus – at least that's what's written on the branch tag. She searches with her eyes for some place to sit, as she needs to gather her thoughts. She needs to determine how she's feeling, because she's feeling so many different things on so many different levels.

She has known Dan Somers for close on seven years, and has been married and living with him for almost five. A long time by anyone's reckoning. She doesn't know what to think about Ena's murder, and him being labelled as a suspect – he is usually quite mild-mannered and easy company. She only ever saw him riled up once, but she witnessed enough in that incident to make her aware that she wouldn't like to walk across his shadow too often. It was one of those incidents that erupt out of nothing – a simple shove in a shopping mall, quite by accident. A Latino. My, but he was one uppity little fella, dingly-dangly from imitation gold hanging off him, earrings and a lip ring. Early twenties with a poor growth of moustache.

He said, rearing up on the toes of his blue sneakers, 'Watch what the fuck you doin, man – you blind *and* fat and stupid?'

Dan apologised. 'Sorry, it was an accident.'

'What you looking at me like that for – like I was a dead skunk or something? Boy, I could pump in your ugly mother-fuckin' ass – do you know who I am?'

The pup. She was about to give him a measure of her tongue when Dan said, 'I said I was sorry – now you need to run along, while you've still got legs to hold you up.'

She couldn't see Dan's eyes from where she stood, but the other man saw enough in them for him to heed that advice. He took a couple of steps backward, fear showing a high wattage in his eyes. He turned about and headed along his way, jeans hanging under the curve of his ass. There'd been an atmosphere of something about to happen, a sort of sizzling electricity. The scene appeared frozen and then it was gone. People looked on, like her, not knowing exactly what they'd just witnessed, knowing only that there had been a heightened expectancy of a ticking bomb about to explode.

Why hadn't she seen any of this coming? she asks herself. She had thought Dan a good man, if complex, attentive to her needs mostly, but sometimes quite distant from her. By degrees his attentiveness lessened and he became more removed. Now she knows why – he is living in the past, and living there doesn't work for anyone. His illness had, she'd thought, brought them together – now it seems it had merely done so for as long as he had been sick.

Her card reading irked him – now she sees why it did: he considered her a fraud because she hadn't seen the truth about him and his past. Or maybe he was scared that she would find out about his past through the cards, eventually. He had demanded that she give it up: the first real emergence of their differences showed in that demand. She'd read all about Thoth, or Hermes, as the Greeks called him, the creator of the tarot. The deck answers the questions, the interpretations gleaned from a book, from experience, from silence. It works for some people and less well for others.

The sun comes out from behind the cloud and she feels its heat on her forehead. Freckles spoiled her face as a kid – her mom often said it was the sun brought them out. Like it did with weeds. She was forever and a day saying hurtful things. It was the drink talking, Irene believes, and the after effects of her benders. But she never cared much about trying to heal things when she was sober. Told Irene to get over it after she tried to explain how badly she was hurting her and her siblings. She might as well have been talking to a mannequin. Irene had already built hundreds of bridges, and it certainly wasn't getting any easier. The very afternoon that her mother had said that to her, she had hopped on a Greyhound bus for a thousand-mile ride and thereafter she leaped from town to town, surviving on the odd waitressing job. She read her tarot how-to book to pass away the time. She had a few flings with men; those she suspected were turning serious she kicked out of her life. Except for Louis.

This is what has happened, she tells herself, looking into her corralled thoughts: prior to today, Dan has said nothing to her about his plan, nor mentioned his wife being a murder victim, his arrest … nothing about his plan to hit back at his sister, to undo her scheme to con him out of money. What else is he holding back?

10

She's away in the gardens, putting her thoughts into order, he understands. She's hurt that he hadn't confided in her. Wondering if he has more news to deliver.

Himself and Ena had danced their first-ever dance to a slow song called 'Alone Again, Naturally' by Gilbert O'Sullivan. A song he and Irene also happened to like. They kept each other at arm's length. A little shy, but that was only because they were under the eyes of the nuns. The hop ended at 11 p.m. and they walked to her house, sharing a bag of chips overdosed with ketchup and vinegar. She was thinner than Irene, but she had curves. Small-breasted, with a long neck, Ena had a gorgeous smile and had a way of tilting her head that he found adorable and affecting. Her smile used to power up his heart.

She lived in a new council estate built on the town's soccer pitch. Next to a factory that lived for ten years and died a death in the recession of the late seventies. After they'd eaten their chips, they popped gum in their mouths and found a dark corner. She let him put a hand under her bra and he could feel the bottom half of her through her tights and panties. More difficult for her to say 'No', than it was for him to accept it. Mere delay, that's all. Everything came off on her mother's new sofa a week later. Weird. One of the things he remembers most about her house is the clothes. The kitchen was awash with rags. Her mother was a seamstress and that explained part of it, but not all. Weird also, to be inside Ena and listening to her moan in almost the same way as her mother did upstairs with her new man. He didn't know how they were able to look at each other over their bowls of cornflakes.

Maybe they didn't, maybe they never looked at each other in the eye – and maybe that was their problem. Ena hadn't been a virgin; he realised that later. There'd been no show of blood, and a complete absence of nervousness and trepidation before their lovemaking. He got to hear of her reputation after he'd fallen for her.... Much too late for him to frogmarch his heart back to its original setting. Much too late for him not to try and save her, save them.

She had a black rose tattoo above her left ankle and at first sight he'd thought it a splash of black paint. Moving closer to her, to her pointed finger showing it off, he saw how incredibly beautiful it was. Skilfully etched by a true artist, one who knew and loved flowers.

'It's great, it looks great,' he said.

'I saw the tattoo in a *Woman's Way* magazine, and I thought it looked like, I don't know, lovely, but more than that – it made the model look different. She stood out from the other pissed-on looking saplings. And I thought, hmm, I would like that – but a black rose tattoo would stand out better than a red or a white … and I wanted it on my leg, not on my arm like in the pic. A tattoo would show the world that I wasn't like Daddy, Mammy, or any of my family – it would make me unique. One of a kind. Special. Am I right?'

'Definitely.'

'I have something to tell you,' Ena said on that rainy day at a bus shelter.

'What is it?'

'I think I'm in love with you.'

'You think?' he thought. Two small, troubling words.

11

He follows Irene into the gardens. She spots him as he looks around for her. He has on that blue shirt he likes and she doesn't – because it doesn't hide the swell of his stomach, it's too short. His glasses are perched on his head; she thinks it lends him a writerly appearance.

She thinks of his illness, how in the months before the awful discovery, they'd been drifting apart. No major upheavals, just an ice floe fracturing. Now, it is back to fracturing … but unlike the last time, there is a loud noise at the rendering that might yet grow louder.

He sees her and begins his approach, torso leaning forward, right hand buried in his pocket. Satchel over his shoulder. She'd bought him it for his birthday, mail order from Amazon, blue denim material with outer pockets of brown leather. Sixty-six bucks. He'd said he liked it, but she knew he didn't. He was a leather man.

She has decided that she does not like Irish skies. They are too grey; a show of the sun too rare.

'It's nice here, isn't it?' he says, his words softly spoken.

She reads the apology in them, his wish for things between them to be smoothed over, for them not to argue. There's a nick from a razor blade under his chin. He pokes his ear with his little finger, and she turns away from him.

'Would you like to come with me to see the house?' he says gently.

'Not particularly.'

'Oh,' he says.

'I mean what's the point, Dan? What I think doesn't seem to count with you anymore.'

'Don't be like that.'

'I shouldn't have come,' she said, staring at the wishing well.

'No,' he said quietly, 'probably not. It's my fault.'

There's nothing to stop me going home – that sudden thought gives her some comfort.

Irene tries to pinpoint exactly when Dan became so distant. There is a vagueness in a few of his answers to her questions; an irritability when his thoughts are interrupted. He seems lost in his daydreams. She can feel him slipping away from her; he is becoming a stranger, and she knows she is powerless to stop it.

Back at the B&B, after walking to town from the gardens, he stands looking through the beige venetian blinds at the car park. Hands on his hips.

'Dan,' she says.

He raises two slats and leans forward to peer between them. Then he releases them and turns around. The blind quivers behind him; the plastic cord binder taps against the wall.

'Yeah?' he says.

'I'm going out.'

'Out?'

'There's an outlet village. I might have a look around.'

'Whattimeisit?' he says, words pushing together, creating something that reveals his impatience and frustration.

'Five past five.'

'I'm going to the house at seven. Please, come along.'

'Does it have to be at that exact time?'

'Half seven then.'

'Good. That gives me plenty of time.'

Silence.

She drapes a pink cardigan over her forearm. Notices a change in his complexion.

'Are you feeling okay?' she says.

'I think I've got a bit of a flu coming on, is all.'

'You do look a bit greyish.'

She fails to mention how the vein at his temple appears like the root of a tree about to break the surface.

'I'll be grand, Irene – you go on.'

She does not want to go shopping, but she cannot tolerate the brooding atmosphere in the room. The easy chord of live and let lie that had lain between them is no longer harmoniously humming; it is now more of a sharp twanging, sounding serious notes of alarm.

At the retail outlet, she strolls along the streets, paying scant attention to the window displays. Wanders in and out of several shops, for the sake of a change of direction, as she tries to pour concrete into her thoughts, to make them set and own a solid foundation. Right now, entering a restaurant near the children's playground, she feels wind-tossed by a storm she hadn't seen coming.

She orders a risotto of wild mushrooms and a glass of house red. She puts her leather diary and her reading glasses on the table. She always feels uncomfortable dining alone in a restaurant, and it is a worse feeling when almost all of the tables are occupied by two or more people. She is sure they are paying her no attention, but that doesn't wash away the oddball feeling.

She opens her diary. What to write? Her Silver Cross pen won't sit still between thumb and forefinger.

She checks her cell phone for messages, though she has no friends – several close ones have moved away, to different time zones within the States, and they'd gradually lost touch. Another had passed away, and others were associates. She'd left her business cell phone behind her. There were bound to be messages on it from clients booking an appointment for a card or phone reading. She wishes she'd brought it along. But then, she hadn't expected this turn of events. A dreamy-eyed version of walking some historical sites, holding hands, taking in the sun and the fresh air, and building up good memories was where her mind had been. Now everything has changed, and is still changing.

What had she seen in him, in those early days? One of the things she'd noticed about him, that she quite liked, was when socialising with their friends, he spoke little and if his voice was lost in the mix of other voices, a tiny wave in a storm, he would lapse into silence and not speak again until spoken to – she could see his mind wander and often wondered where it brought him. She liked the way he did not feel the need to assert himself, push himself against the grain ... a good listener, a man who held his counsel. She realises how much this image is at odds with the man he may actually be – a man who may have murdered his wife. She feels sick in her stomach. It is, she figures, her hopes falling from the sky and coming to rest as dead bones in her heart.

12

He shaves, examines the mole on his cheek in the mirror. Has it changed colour? Grown by a fraction? Maybe. He dries himself, puts on fresh clothes and boils the kettle to make coffee. Opens a sachet of Nescafé, another of brown sugar, rinses the cup in the bathroom sink.

He sips at his coffee, looking out the window. Earlier, he had seen a young woman getting out of a car. She was foreign looking. He would guess that she was French. She'd dropped her purse and he was about to rap the window to alert her when she copped its absence and retrieved it. Good looking woman, he'd thought, when she bent over. Perfectly rounded....

He finishes his coffee and leaves a note for Irene, telling her he's gone down to the house and to follow if she's interested. He wants her to see it, to share with her the place where he had been reared. He does not know why this is important – she must be confused – for the man she knows is not one who overly believes in the importance of anything.

His mother's ghost walks with him on the way to the house. Brings with her a shakedown of memories – he can hear her voice, picture her so clearly. A tangible ghost. His main memories consists of arguments with her; he remembers how they had argued about nothing and everything and stuff in-between.

Arguing can grow into a habit. His mother's superiority complex blew against the wind chimes of his own natural sensibilities. She said he was a carbon copy of her father, which was about one hundred miles short of being a compliment – a man who wore his socks inside out every day, who had sloppy standards.

She believed you could take the boy out of the council house but not the council house out of the boy. She said it was important to wear money well – and to keep in the right company – the bank manager, the parish priest, the school principal – in with the people who mattered, who could influence things for you. People who could open doors, bypass red tape, get things done and done far quicker than would happen for an ordinary person, who, after all, needed keeping in their place – how could society hope to function if they weren't?

His mother was old-fashioned. She liked the old traditions, the old ways of doing things. The notion of women wanting to leave their children with strangers so they could go to work? Such nonsense. A woman's place was in the home, looking after it, rearing her children – that's what the Lord intended. And running off to England to murder babies, those ... those ... *women* ... should be shot at dawn. How could they do such a terrible thing? These people were not women at all. Not a moral stitch to their souls, none of them. Breeding. Lack of. It was blatantly obvious. 'You wouldn't see one of mine come in,' she was fond of saying, 'and say she was pregnant or had gotten a trollop in that condition. I'd break the legs from under them, if they did – but they wouldn't dare, because they knew what would happen. Yet, you hear so much of this sort of thing happening, families of good class brought low by the low. Not here, it better not ... it never would.'

He had thought she'd worked herself into a state over scenes yet to evolve, that most likely never would, speaking against them as though warning God against visiting them upon her.

She had missed his father, and had never gotten over his passing. She would sometimes smile at the picture of him on the mantle – often recall the time when two tinkers called to the door to sell a telly 'chape' and oh didn't he bring them in, and tested the telly, in spite of her saying for him not to. A mighty picture for sure, the young scruff said. He ran them off when they refused to drop the price, though he was sorely tempted to buy it, for the price was reasonable and the TV new. They returned a half hour later to say they'd accept his offer and he couldn't resist the temptation. He told them to leave it in the sitting room and paid them. Of course, when the blaggards and the stink of them had gone, he plugged in the TV. There was no sign of life in it. A dud. She said that he had lost the head completely. She had never saw him so mad in her life.

He is drawn out of his recollections by the chaos that greets him at the house. It stands, redbrick, behind a copse of old sentinel pine, up a lick of worn tarmac, about a quarter mile outside of town. Five rooms upstairs, six down. A blue garage door hangs by the last of its hinges. The roofs of two garden sheds reveal mostly bare board and tiny scraps of mineral felt. Weeds prosper, a few violets, the sole hint of the garden's better days.

The last occupants had left about a month ago. Letters and fliers clutter the hair mat. He brushes them to the side with two sweeps of his foot. As he is doing this, the smell announces its presence. Mould, damp, dead plants. The walls are a lime-green, blistered here and there, and there are ghostly clean patches where paintings used to hang.

He enters room after room downstairs. Nostalgia rushes to embrace with a flood of memories. He is shocked a little by the physical emptiness he finds in each room, though there is furniture, there are ornaments.

The interior is not as bad as the exterior indicated. Clean, but old. Archaic electrical sockets, a Stanley range that looks smoked out and in need of replacing. Each step of the stairs moans under the fall of his feet. He is on the landing when he hears the front door open. For a moment he thinks it is Irene. And in the same moment, realises that it can't be. She hasn't got a key.

'Teresa?' he calls.

'Billy J.'

'I'm upstairs.'

'Can I come on up?'

'Sure. Where's Teresa?'

'Outside.'

He hadn't heard a car pull up. Perhaps the creaking boards had disguised the engine noise.

He enters the smallest of the bedrooms and goes to the window. Looks through smeared glass at a red Nissan Micra, at his sister smoking and talking on her phone.

'I think you know why I'm here,' Billy J. says, standing in the doorway.

'You're going to ask me for a favour, right?'

Billy J. nods. 'Maybe beg is a more fitting word.'

Dan thinks his brother-in-law appears done in. He looks even worse than he did at the restaurant. He's deathly pale, and worry lines reveal the inner hauntings. He is not, he reckons, having an easy time of it with Teresa. His sister isn't one to give people a rest. Dan feels a tinge of admiration for Billy J. – he had stuck with Teresa through the highs and lows. When his horses were all but tripping themselves up on the racecourse, when he couldn't train a winner if every horse in the race was his, he'd to contend with her making him feel smaller than he already did.

'Don't beg,' Dan said.

13

I never could bring myself to tell Young Benny that I saw his mother being killed. I still occasionally experienced nightmares about her blood showing red in my eyes and working its way inside me for years after the accident. I kept seeing the facecloth on the sink in the shopkeeper's bathroom as well. It had been blue and looked as though someone had just dipped it in a vat of red dye.

The evening of the accident, Daddy got fed up listening to me crying and lashed out. I stopped crying, because I didn't want to feel his knuckles ram hard into my bone a second time. I didn't sleep. I cried under my blankets; even in that comforting heat I could hear the wind blowing and the squealing of brakes. I imagined the tears falling were of blood. In the morning, Mammy said, 'Jesus, what's that mark on your wrist?' A set of teeth imprints. I'd bitten there to stop myself crying out for her in the middle of the night.

Young Benny went sick from work with jaundice for a while, and Luigi gave me extra shifts. He'd gotten a jukebox installed and I liked to listen to the music while I worked. Dr Hook was my favourite group and I used to think it sad about the guy ringing Sylvia and getting to speak with her mother, who must have been a right cow not to tell her daughter that she was wanted. Sounded like something Mammy would do. If she ever did that to me, I would be fit to be tied. Took me a while to realise that maybe Sylvia hadn't wanted to talk to the guy. Stuff like that always came late to me.

The evenings were quiet in Luigi's early on in the week. He looked worn out and his fingers were crowded with rings. A gold chain dripped from his neck. He smelled of Brut aftershave, grease, burger meat, and onions. Fish, too. Cod. He was sad but a cheery sort of sad – he smiled through whatever ached inside him.

Most of the customers were fine, they just wanted to buy their food and go home. The picture-house crowd would come in a little after 10.30 and order, usually burgers and chips. While they waited, I'd get to hear what show had been on, if it was any good. The pub crowd would come in a little later and I didn't like them very much. They talked dirty and complained about everyone except themselves. Red faces flushed from drinking, they'd press close to the counter, putting more salt and vinegar on top of food already over salted. Some would openly belch. They smoked, nearly all of them. So the little chipper with the black and red tile floors, the jukebox, boiling oil, smoking and beer belch, reminded me of a thieves' den I'd seen on telly in a Sunday afternoon matinee. Pictures during which Mammy could always be relied upon to say, 'They don't make them like that anymore.'

As compressed an atmosphere as the chipper was sometimes, there was never much trouble. The worse incident was when a tinker threw a bag of chips at me and called me a little hoor. That he'd ride the life out of me if I didn't give him a bag of fresh chips. Luigi calmed him down by offering him a cigarette and replacement chips. I was always afraid of tinkers after that, because I never understood why he had reared up at me. Maybe he thought

I'd given him a bad look, and maybe I did, unbeknownst to myself. He wore raggy clothes and a grimy cloth cap. Unopened bottles of beer squatted in his jacket pockets. His name was Poncho McDonagh and he lived with his family in a caravan out by the Curragh, on the road to the cross-country course. One of his daughters came now and then to my school. She always had a snotty nose and smelled of burned sticks but I never minded her sitting beside me. I think we both had the worse attendance record in the class.

The nuns never really bothered with me anyway, unless they wanted to let off steam or make a point – they stuck mostly to teaching the brightest girls and the ones they knew had a bit of standing in the community. God was out the window with me, and that drove them to despair. I couldn't say that to them outright, but they knew I was a non-believer. One nun, Sister Roe, liked to fire a question to the stupid ones in our class, questions she knew we wouldn't have the answer to. She would finish every class by asking if we had any questions. I had one, one that I had been thinking about for a long time.

She picked my hand out of all the ones raised.

'Yes, Philomena, what is your question?'

'Sister, if Jesus told the Apostles to pray the Our Father – well, why do we need to pray to Jesus and Mary and the saints? He said for us to pray to the Father.'

I was curious. That's all. It wasn't a try-to-catch-out-the-teacher question. I wanted to know.

She said nothing. Touched the rim of her wimple. The others in the class turned their heads to look back at me, as though I was after landing myself in a pile of trouble and wanted to get a good look at me, before I was punished – because I was bound not to look the same afterwards.

'If you were coming to class on a regular basis, Miss Tierney, you wouldn't have had to ask that silly question.'

Then the bell rang.

Luigi got kidney stones and he was going to be in hospital for six weeks. Benny and I had to run the takeaway in his absence. It was summertime and I was off school. It was the best time of my life. I didn't have to get up for school and I was able to save a little money in the post office. Not much, but it was something. I didn't feel poor. I was poor, I knew, but I was doing something about it. Seventeen, nearly. I was after getting tall and my breasts had shot out almost overnight. Still pale and pimply faced, though, so I decided to stop eating Luigi's food. But spots can be hard to shift and they were red, a sore red, and they made me think of the accident. Got so I found it hard to look at myself in a mirror.

Many things brought me back to the accident.

Still had the nightmares and they'd gotten really bad when I had my first period, because the show of blood brought me to the windy day. Usually, I felt like screaming – but I bottled up all that screaming and let it rage around inside me. I drank some of Mammy's hidden supply of vodka and that quietened the storm.

Around about the time I started drinking, Mammy started up her business full time as a seamstress and she had more people coming to her for alterations. A few men started to arrive too, looking for a waist to be let free, or a leg to be turned up, and for hours she would hunch over the Philips she'd bought on tick. It was a holy mess, the house, with clothes everywhere. She could remember who owned what, though, she never lost sight of that or how much was owed to her. Later, she fell for a client called Harry Wolfe and he took a shine to me and my sister. I didn't like the way he looked at my brother, Tommy, either. I got them away, to live with my aunts, who all lived around the town. Mammy didn't mind – she only worried about Daddy coming home and catching her rocking their bed with Harry. Then Daddy died and she had no worry.

Young Benny and I, we did what Luigi asked of us: to hold the fort until he was better. The town never put a statue in the square for us – we brought the cheeseburger to town. Introduced too, onion rings and battered sausages.

Dr Hook had other hits apart from that song about poor Sylvia and after we'd closed for the night, Young Benny and I would dance to the songs we played from the money he'd short-changed some customers out of. We danced until maybe two in the morning. Then we'd leave and he'd walk me a bit of the way home.

Stuff we talked about we never shared with anyone else. I learned he'd been married for a couple of years, Beth was her name. That he had a son in England. He told me about his mother, Bella. What had happened to her. An accident about ten years old by the time we spoke about it. I listened, but my mind was pushing him along. He lived alone in a new flat. He was after selling his mother's house and was planning to head to England. Manchester, he said, where he was going to invest in a takeaway shop. Beth was always looking for him back, but he wasn't on for going. He made it sound like he was the crown jewels or something – and he didn't like his father-in-law either. Said Owen Noctor was a dirty and dangerous prick, a rip-off merchant, and that he'd do him in if he ever got the chance.

'Do you want to come back to the flat for a drink?' he said a couple of weeks later, after we'd closed up for the night and had spent an hour joking and talking.

His arm was around my waist and it felt good. Warm. Comfy, exciting. Earlier, he'd slipped his corduroy jacket over my shoulders, even though I'd said I wasn't cold.

Young Benny had jet-black hair, and a scar under his eye that made him look tougher than he actually was. A buzz of excitement surged through me. I couldn't believe this. He was much older, but we got along well. We had some laughs.

'I won't mess you about,' he said, 'you're too young … how old are you anyway?'

'I'm old enough.'

I guess saying that was the start to another set of events.

14

He couldn't, or wouldn't, wait for her. It occurs to Irene not to bother going to see the house, to instead lie on the bed for a little while and chill. But he would sulk and his sulky moods are infectious. And she did not want to spend her 'holiday' in a foul mood – what sort of memories would that make for?

Bad ones at the moment, that's without doubt.

She changes shoes. Walking doesn't bother her; she walked miles every other day back home, along a leafy road that traipses through a forest. She is thinking about getting a dog to accompany her, because there are stretches of the route often empty, and only God knows what sort of monsters could be lurking – these days, one can't be careful enough. She likes Labradors. She'd hoped Dan would have taken the hint for her birthday but he let on not to have understood. He'd deflected her hint by suggesting she buy herself a little .38 revolver – it would prove a cheaper investment in the long haul. So she had made up her mind to buy a little black Labrador puppy for herself and surprise him with it – but decided not to in the end, as she didn't want Dan setting up camp in her ear.

A breeze pushes at her back as she walks down the main street, past shops permanently closed and others with about as much cheer as a cell on Death Row. She'd seen cheerier-looking tombstones. And the people don't smile. Their faces grim, strained, as though they'd found all their hunting traps empty and none left to check. She sees her old self in some of them – days when her tomorrows looked like they'd happened yesterday.

At the house, well … she has to stand back and give it a good look over. He'd never said it was this big. *Then again, the pig hadn't told me much about anything.*

Lovely sized grounds. She adores redbrick, finds it charming, old worldly. Dilapidated – the windows are of old wooden sash. The gardens are grown wild and, she says to herself, 'Are they mushrooms?' Magic – yes – she confirms on closer inspection. She knows her mushrooms. Her aunt used to brew them for tea. Irene only ever had a single sip. It had tasted, she'd imagined, about as bad as drinking water sieved through one of her granpappy's socks.

Teresa is smoking, leaning her behind against the boot of a rented red Micra, ankles crossed, her brown coat buttoned up to the neck. Her arms are folded, face like a pissed-upon weed.

'Hi,' Irene says, pasting on a smile and injecting softness into her tone.

'Hi.'

'They're inside?'

Teresa nods. Her shoulders pent up so high they could keep a circus tent pitched. Her lips seem to be clutching at the cigarette. Irene had witnessed scenes like this in the hospital – anxious loved ones waiting to hear what news would come barging through the double doors.

'Yeah, they're in there,' Teresa says.

'I should give them a minute?'

'If you wouldn't mind.'

'Not in the least.'

Silence.

Irene says, 'You were never very close, you two, were you?'

'Is it that obvious?'

'It is, yes.'

Teresa sighs long and hard, clutches the cigarette and exhales.

'He's a changed man since he landed here,' Irene says quietly, probing a little.

'He'd a tough time after Ena died – that's his wife's name, he's told you the whole story by now, I guess.'

Irene nods, though it's a lying nod. *What is the whole story?* Part of her wants to correct Teresa for referring to Ena as Dan's current wife, but lets it drift.

'Did you know her?' Irene asks.

'Sort of – she didn't have a good reputation. She liked her men, her drink and I'm not going to judge her. I would have back then. Now, Jesus, if we don't get a break where money is concerned, Billy J. is going to gaol. That's *our* bad reputation. We've nowhere left to run – here or in New Zealand.'

Irene says, 'Did the police ever find out who killed Ena? Who was their prime suspect?'

Teresa dwells on the question, as though judging what size portion she should cut. 'I think they did and they didn't – the word was strong that Dan was the prime suspect.'

'Was?' Irene presses. Dan has already told her this, but it feels as though she's listening to fresh news, coming off someone else's lips. And it stings her all over again.

'I'm sure he told you that much.'

'I–'

'Speak to your husband,' Teresa says.

Irene winces at the sudden and unexpected slash of claw.

15

A big ask, a hard ask for Billy J. Every pore in his face looks like its spilling beads of perspiration. He is on the verge of tears. Dan rocks forward and back on his toes, wishing Billy J. would stand aside and allow him space to leave the bedroom.

'We're so on our uppers,' Billy J. says. 'I hate myself for hitting on you like this – I feel like shit, you know – but I know you and Teresa – well – it's been left to me to do the crawling.'

'I'll think on it,' Dan says.

'I'm not even going to lie and tell you it's a loan, Dan. I won't insult you. There's no way I'm going to be able to repay you. I don't think I'll even live long enough to do that.'

'I said I'll think on it.'

Billy J. bobs his head several times and scratches his chin.

'I understand,' he said, 'you need to speak with Irena, yeah?'

'Irene.'

'Irene. Yes, I understand – of course.'

'Not necessarily. I doubt if she'd want anything to do with this whole business.'

16

Young Benny had an upstairs flat. There was a Honda 50 in the hall and a beat-up washing machine under the stairwell. A clotheshorse with socks draped over the rods. Bare concrete stairs led the way to a locked door the same colour as a coffin lid.

'Is that your bike?' I asked, touching the handlebar, squeezing a lever.

'Was,' he said. 'I'm holding it for a guy, till he has the spondulicks to pay for it.'

He patted my bum and moved his hand to the small of my back, nudging me to begin the climb. At the top, he opened the door and ushered me in, saying, 'Welcome to the Chateau Young Benny.'

It was clean. No clothes lying about, nor noise from a sewing machine, nor cigarette smoke clouding the air. A calendar hung on the pantry door – 'October 1983' in bold above a photograph of a red deer in a misty wood. He'd marked the dates on which he'd to work in Luigi's.

He said, 'Sit down,' and I sat on a two-seater couch with foam spilling out at the armrests.

He put on the portable telly and the screen came to life with a rolling black line. Young Benny adjusted the aerial, said it was a waste of time – the telly took moods. Usually, the picture was perfect. I didn't believe that. I think he had gotten used to the roll. Video cassettes were stacked on a shelf in the telly's wooden stand. He saw me looking and said they were pirated copies a mate of his brought back from Spain. Shite quality.

Next he got the heater going. Left it on a single bar.

He said, 'Any more and the smell of gas would flip your stomach.'

I was nervous and I could tell that he was too. He traced the tip of his forefinger along my arm, at the scars that had long healed. Stanley knife scrapes, I said to him. He counted off six.

'Just the right arm?' he said.

'Yes.'

'Why?'

'Why I sliced myself – used to?'

'A-ha.'

'I don't know.'

I did – but what should I have said? That I was excavating his mother's blood?

'But you're finished with doing that?' he said.

'I'm long finished with doing that – so relax.'

We sat in silence and then I said I was thinking of getting a tattoo of a black rose. He said two black roses would be unique. He said it quietly – and I sensed he was hiding his real thoughts, but it was typical of me to be wondering if people were saying other stuff along with what I could hear them say. I did get the black rose tattoo later – dainty with slender stems. I used to spray perfume on it to give the petals a scent, and I used also to wonder what my rose would look like when I got old.

Sitting beside me, he handed me a bottle of lager.

'Hungry?' he asked.

I shook my head, looked down at the toes of my trainers. The white rims were scuffed. I wore no socks. I kicked the trainers off.

'You're shameless,' he said, 'showing off your naked feet.'

'Cheers,' I said, leaning my bottle toward his for the clink.

'Cheers,' he said.

We drank at the same time, his bottle jarred a little against his teeth and I hoped it wasn't the eyetooth that he sometimes complained about. Young Benny raised his behind and felt his pocket for a lighter. Took a pack of cigarettes from his shirt pocket and lit up, handed me a cig to puff, and I did. I think he expected me to cough, but smoking, though I hadn't formed the habit, wasn't a new experience for me.

I could smell the rankness of his armpits and the reek on his clothes from the chipper. But I smelt like that too. I loved his hands, the fine dark hair on the backs of them, the way the knuckles resembled little hills, the veins like underground streams.

'Can I ask you something, Ena?'

'Go ahead.'

'Do you have a boyfriend?'

I was aware of the real meaning to his question – would he be my first?

'No. But I've had boys interested in me,' I shrugged. 'The thing is, they're all so, you know, bloody immature and silly.'

A lie, but I didn't want him thinking that no one was interested. One lad had said I resembled a prickless altar boy.

Charlie Potter wanted to be my boyfriend, but I couldn't stand the sight of his buckteeth – he was nice, but no thanks. I told him my mother said I was too young to be dating. 'Just to the pictures,' Charlie insisted, 'Jesus sake.' But I shook my head, saying Mammy would kill me if she found out. Mothers are born to be blamed.

Young Benny slid his hand around my neck, pressed his hand against my upper arm and drew me to him. He felt so warm. I could hear his heart beating through his shirt. He stroked my neck with the tips of his fingers. Draws that made me feel special and were so lovely. I didn't want him to stop doing that.

I looked up at him and he kissed me on the lips.

I could see the hunger rage wild in his eyes – bright shiny jewels. He said, 'Not here.'

He got to his feet, took my hand and led me into his bedroom. I knew what was going to happen and I didn't mind it in the least.

17

Irene could live in a house like this, if it was done up properly. But it would eat money to make it even someway habitable. Might make better financial sense to knock it down and rebuild. She susses this before even getting to see upstairs.

The two men join her in the kitchen. She says hello to Billy J. and he gives a tight smile in response. Merely shoots a glance toward her husband, enough to make him aware she is on the warpath.

'I better be going,' Billy J. says, sounding as though he would give anything for a reason to stay, or to at least leave with good news.

Dan says flatly, 'Okay.'

'I'll see myself out,' he says, his eyes on Dan, who keeps his back to them.

Irene waits until the footsteps recede and the door closes out, before saying, 'What's going on?'

'He begged me to reconsider the house sale.'

'Will you turn about and talk to me, for frig's sake – what the hell has gotten into you lately?'

He faces her.

'Tell me,' she asks.

'I said I'd think about it, the house sale.'

He leans his back against the kitchen worktop. Crosses his ankles.

'What do you think?' he says.

'Spacious and smelly.'

'It is. But I was asking for your thoughts on the whole shebang to do with Teresa and Billy J.'

'Cut them the deal – it's probably the last dealings you'll ever have with them.'

'Hmm,' he says.

A magpie lands on the shed roof.

Irene feels a headache coming on.

He says, 'It's going back on the market – it was never off it – I just wanted to let them know they were trying to diddle the wrong person.'

Cruel, but then his sister had been cruel to him. His appetite for forgiveness is generally anorexic, Irene thinks. She can hardly fault him, as she too finds it hard to forgive people certain things.

'So, you've decided to keep me in the loop about what's going on in that brain of yours,' Irene says. 'I was asking myself just who the hell you were. Is that what a blast of Irish air does to you – puts the A into asshole?'

He holds up his hands in a show of mock surrender. 'Sorry – but I'm processing a lot of stuff, a lot of it I'd forgotten about, Irene. Pushed to the background … buried….'

'What gives with you and Teresa anyway – where did the bad blood between you come from?'

She isn't sure if it's the thing to ask, for in her experience not much of anything is required in order for people to fall out with each other.

'Oh, she told the guards I'd asked her to give me an alibi for the night Ena was attacked … that first time.'

'First time?'

'A couple of weeks before she was killed, she was badly beaten up.'

What the … what the hell is he telling me? That he beat up his wife?

Suddenly, a sweeping sensation brings a coldness to her tummy. Who is this man?

'Gee … you need to talk to me about this, Dan, all of it. This is too serious for me to go painting by the numbers you dish out whenever you feel like it.'

He sights. 'Let's go into the garden – I can't talk here – the air – the smell – the history.…'

'Okay,' she says, going to him and taking his hand, because the sunlight is highlighting his well of tears, and the ache in his voice sounds like the slow tearing of a page from a copybook.

A thought cuts her, such is the jolt of fresh awareness. He gave his first wife a hiding.

She lets go of his hand.

18

His mother, after learning he was dating, and not just dating Ena, but seriously so, did a freakie in the kitchen. He'd stormed out, chased by language he'd never heard his mother use before. She must have said 'Jesus Christ' about a dozen times and invectives rained down upon his head. She was beside herself with rage.

'If only your father was alive,' she 'd said.

He'd looked at her in surprise. He and Teresa feared her temper much more than they ever did their father's. She was the one who meted out physical, mental and emotional punishment.

He'd learned something from her, he supposed, thinking how he'd strung his sister along to make her suffer.

Irene wanted answers. About Ena. Would he ever be done with his first wife?

19

After we'd done it, he slid off me. It had hurt me a little, not much. There wasn't much joy in it for me, but Young Benny behaved as though he'd landed on cloud nine. He was gentle at first but when he got going he forgot himself and pushed my knees right up to my ears. When he came, he panted like an old horse, such a wheeze in his lungs, and I think he must have dropped every drop of sweat in him on top of me. Because he was a little heavy around the belly, he leaned his torso upwards with his hands either side of my ears. He looked deep into my eyes and I closed mine, not liking that, not liking the feeling that he was taking something from me – I didn't want to see the giving of myself to him in his eyes. Only the taking. I could have pushed him off me at that point – thought about it – but the notion rolled away as he thrust deep and I felt the awakenings of pleasure. What with the chip oil leaking through our pores, we were greased-up pigs.

The room was tiny and my side of the bed was against the wall. There were leak stains on the ceiling, curiously shaped.

'Okay?' he said.

'Sure. You?' I said, easing from the bed, seeing the patch of blood on the sheet – it added an arctic touch to my heart.

'Yeah, yeah. Where are you going?'

'The loo.'

'Are you okay, chick? You look like you've seen a ghost.'

'I'm fine. Don't call me chick – I'm not a chick.'

'Don't leave the flat, Ena, it's too late.'

He just wanted to sleep now – that was in his tone.

'I won't,' I said.

I sat on the toilet and let the cold air dry me. He was running out of me. I didn't like the smell. I peed and folded over some leafs of toilet paper and put them in my knickers when I got back into bed. Young Benny was sleeping. I turned off the light, lay on my back and looked into the darkness, eating the silence.

In the morning, I woke to find him gone from the bed and the flat. I took a shower, made tea, and waited for him to return. It was after midday and I was hoping Mammy wouldn't have gone to the guards to report me missing. I should have called and told her I'd stayed over with a friend. I could have done that from the phone in Luigi's office. I was never much good at thinking about doing the proper thing. I was fed up waiting for Young Benny and I left after I'd finished drinking my tea. I like my tea black and sugary, which was good, as Young Benny had no milk in his fridge. In fact, he had nothing in his fridge.

Mammy remained silent when I stepped into the sitting room. She was a hump of temper behind her sewing machine. When I saw the clothes strewn everywhere, I was glad I'd stayed away – don't people ever think of washing their clothes before handing them in for alterations?

The machine whirred to a stop.

'Where were you last night – and don't you fucking dare lie to me,' she said, staring at a zip on a pair of grey jeans.

'I stayed over with Young Benny.'

'Foster?'

'A-ha.'

Her face darkened. It was as if whisps of black cloud had come round from the back of her head and flanked her nose.

'Nothing happened,' I said quickly.

'Really?'

'Did he use…?'

Young Benny hadn't used a rubber.

'If you get yourself pregnant, I'll fucking brain you, Ena, if that was possible, because I swear to Christ I think the sheep on the Curragh have more sense than you.'

Young Benny went cool on me then. Kept his distance at work. Acted as if he was preoccupied and in a bad mood. I got so thick with him that I almost blurted out that his mother had kissed me with her blood. I treated him the way he treated me, but I really wanted to talk with him, hug him, and feel his fingers dance on my neck and arms. When I had my period, I wouldn't tell him. I wanted him to ask. He never did. The day after Luigi arrived into the chipper unannounced, he was gone. England, I heard, with his wife Beth, to try to make a proper go of things. He had his mother's house money and more, the bastard.

Luigi beckoned me into his office. He was a big man in a small space. He looked dreadful. 'Ena, I have something to discuss with you. Something very serious.'

I went to sit. He said I was to stand.

'Yes,' I said, feeling a bit panicky. Nothing good was coming out of Luigi's mouth, I could tell.

'The takings – the business is down a lot of money,' he said.

Jesus, Mary. 'I didn't take it. I swear.'

I was genuinely shocked.

'Benny didn't make any lodgements into the bank – and he's vanished.'

He was teary and had a haunted look of disappointment – he'd been badly let down by people he'd trusted when most vulnerable, seriously ill, and, 'fucked,' as he went on to tell me.

He let out this long sigh. His hand went into a fist. Like a lump hammer. His knuckles were small white humps. He thumped the table – pens went everywhere, his invoice book, loose change.

I began to cry.

20

Being in the garden doesn't make him eager to talk. He says again there were too many memories in the house – he would prefer to talk later, at the B&B. A gut instinct assumes control, the one she'd initially ignored. Irene refuses to let him off the hook.

The trees seem to shout their agitation with him; they stir and dance in a sudden gust of wind that quickly falls to silence.

'Why did you want Teresa to lie for you, Dan?'

'I said–'

'No, let's clear this up now. Did you beat the crap out of your wife?'

He blanches.

'I want to hear you say it, Dan.'

'I never laid a hand on you, did I?'

'We're not talking about me.'

'All that happened before we met.'

She's never seen him in such distress, not even when they'd sat in that doctor's office and listened to him pour out the results of Dan's medical tests.

'If it's nothing got to do with me, then why I am in this sad little town? This is supposed to be a vacation, but instead, it's turning into a really bad tour – I have to be honest with you, Dan. I'm pretty damn sore about this.'

'I—'

'I'm not done talking – you want to postpone telling me the tale, but what I'm saying is this – you've already postponed it for far too long.'

He put his hands to his face and then holds them out as if he's a frigging pope. An urge to have a cigarette comes upon her like a tsunami.

'Okay,' he says, his voice breaking.

A rise of traffic noise, that quickly passes.

'Before we start,' he says, 'I ... it wasn't a habit, I want you to believe me about that.'

It is going to choke him, she understands, to paint this particular canvas for her.

He begins, avoiding her gaze, by saying they had argued over her spending the last of their money on a silver bangle. She said she loved the Celtic knot design at its ends. Showed it to him and said it was the last one Catherine had on her stall – Catherine was an aunt of hers into handcraft, who sold at the Thursday market. It was too big for Ena's wrist and slid halfway down her hand. In a temper, he grabbed it from her, went outside their flat and threw it over the cathedral wall, into the grounds with the tower. She called him a bastard and ran up the laneway, with the intention of entering the grounds and retrieving it – but the old green gates were locked. The deacon's house was close by and she rang the doorbell. She and the old deacon must have spent a couple of hours searching for the bangle but to no avail – she saw the deacon's daughter wearing it at a disco a week later. And got it back.

He paused. She told him to continue, to get back to his alibi request.

'Anyway, she sulked and she ... she went off with a fella – you know about that sort of stuff – I mentioned it – and

I got so thick I followed her. She used to see this guy for money, you know, and walk home alone after the business transaction. I went up to her from behind and I hit her and kept hitting her ... if I hadn't stopped, I would probably have killed her. But I did stop. I was stopped, because someone heard her scream and came running. I ran ... I ran and kept running.'

Silence.

He adds, 'That's it. She ended up in dock for a day, needed a couple of stitches under her ear, and two weeks later, she was dead. No one came running to help her.'

So intense is the silence he thinks nature is listening. There's not even a roll of traffic, a peep of birdsong, a stir of branch.

Irene says, 'What else? This alibi you asked her for – I'm reading something into that.'

'She didn't give me one, remember? I always kind of admired her for not doing it, and....'

'Go on.'

'She gave me one later,' he says, very quietly.

'Let me guess. For the night Ena was murdered.'

'Yes.'

'You asked her for one that night, too?'

'I was a lead suspect. But I didn't ask her, no – my mother did.'

'Frigs sake, Dan. Did you kill Ena?'

Nature is straining its ears.

'In a way, but not directly.'

'Sweet Lord,' Irene says. 'Mafia godfathers say that sort of shit, Dan.'

'It wasn't a hit, Irene – what do you think I am?'

'I don't know – I have no idea, that's the Lord's honest truth. I thought listening to you would help me figure it out, but you're a right sinkhole, Dan, a right friggin sinkhole. I can't get a handle on you at all.'

'Read your cards,' he says, huffed.

'Oh, like never before.'

21

Sick to the depths of his heart, that's what I thought of Young Benny as I peeled potatoes for the slicer machine. Mid-morning and the chipper smelt of cold chip oil, washed potatoes and Blisteze ointment on my cold sore. I was run down. Disheartened too, because I never took Young Benny to be a king-size rat. I missed all of his rat signals. There had to be some that I should have read – he'd thought nothing of me, our dancing to the jukebox songs, his/our scheme of skimming change. He said we were like Robin Hood and Maid Marian: we stole from the loaded and those who wouldn't give you the steam from their cat's piss. Only I didn't steal – I should have squared him on that. I did it accidentally, okay, one time. He saw me and probably thought we were a match for each other.

My blood heated over with the thinking of how he'd rode me – it was mean of him to pretend he cared for me, mean of him to rob Luigi and mean to let the suspicion fall to the eejit, me. Luigi stared hard at a point above my head when I told him I knew nothing about the takings. He said he would give me the benefit of the doubt, but his tone held only a lick of benefit.

I should have sussed the sort Young Benny was as soon as he piped up and mentioned the skimming racket. He smiled at the people he cheated and spoke in a friendly way.

That was hint enough – smiling as he stole, looking them in the eye. 'Ah, Young Benny's sound,' customers said to me after asking had he quit. Not many knew what he had done, the ones who asked after him obviously didn't – the ones who did said nothing about his absence.

I should have said it to him about my drenching with his mother's blood. Though he probably wouldn't care – he'd probably shake his head in that stupid way he thinks is cool and so Steve McQueen-like, like in *The Getaway*. We'd watched the film together – he'd rented it from Tits Dolan and a blue film I pretended to like, but didn't. It was disgusting and Young Benny wanted me to suck him but I said no way. I felt bad about not doing it, but I'm glad now that I'd stuck to my guns. I'd sooner put a toilet plunger in my mouth and call myself a Chinese name, Shit in Teeth or something, than have anything more to do with Young Benny.

Mammy put the squeeze on to see if Young Benny had given me a share of the loot. She also gave me the benefit of the doubt when I said he hadn't.

'Not a farthing, Ena?' she said, piling clothes into a shopping bag.

The house had been painted. It smelled of gloss paint and old rags. She was trying, though. I think she was trying to get the kids back living with her, but no way with Freako Wolfe still on the prowl with his I'll-ride-youse-all eyes. He came and went. I wished him ten heart attacks.

'Nothing, not a cent,'

'That's men for you,' she said, tying a knot and throwing the bag on top of others.

'No, Mammy, that's a rat for you.'

She smiled. I could almost see her thoughts – a few weeks ago, I'd thought the galaxy shone out of Young Benny's pimply posterior.

The summer pushed along and I worked four or sometimes five nights a week. The nights I was off, I would meet up with a couple of my friends, Hazel Rochford and Gilly Maher; they were a great laugh, but it got so they were leaning on me to buy them fags and cider. They'd come in the odd night begging with their eyes for me to take the hint and feed them burgers and chips, a cola – they were wearing Young Benny's type of coat and I told them to fuck off with themselves. Users, I called them.

Mammy was getting notes home from the nuns – I was facing into doing my Leaving Cert the next year and needed to improve on my attendance record and brush up on my studying. I wanted to leave school but Mammy said I could do what I like when I reached my eighteenth birthday – she'd made a promise to some saint that she'd keep me in school until then, if he granted her a favour. I had to suffer for a saint doing her a favour. I half-wished I was pregnant, almost.

Luigi hired another man the same age as Young Benny. He had tattoos of bluebirds on his bulging forearms and long black hair he kept tied back. He used to visit Mammy to have his trousers let out and whatever. His belly was huge. Mammy cracked up with she heard my nickname for him, 'Mirror Mickey', because he must have to hold one in front of there, if he wanted to see it.

His real name was Don Lally and his thin lips looked like they'd been worn away to give them a cutting edge, like the sea gives to rocks, sharpens them enough to slice a hull open. I picked up that he was cruel. But I told myself I could be as wrong about him as I had been about Young Benny.

Sometimes, a Dr Hook ballad oozed from the jukebox and I'd lapse into sadness and silence. When I was mopping the floor after closing time, Mirror Mickey sailed from behind the counter and felt my arse as he passed by. A slow feel. I clocked him with the wet filthy mop and Luigi erupted in laughter. Mirror Mickey laughed too, but nervously. I knew then that Young Benny had talked about us – but I wasn't certain – maybe I was paranoid. But maybe it was too much of a coincidence too – that's how Young Benny started his tricks, by grabbing my butt, as if it was part of him, as if he had a right to it. Mirror Mickey, his laughter was fused with anger. He was doing his utmost not to let it show in front of Luigi.

After he finished laughing, Luigi wagged his finger at Don, and said, 'No more.'

I liked Luigi. A lot of people didn't, for reasons I never got to hear – but he never did anything wrong by me. And he gave me the benefit of the doubt, against his better judgement.

22

She ignores him when he says he's going to stay in the bar for a bit. She leaves. He's a mouth ulcer on the roof of his mouth and it is more worrying and aggravating than painful. He is sure he'd gotten it from sucking on a bon bon. He'd bought a bag of the white powered sweets from a kiosk at the train station – acting on a flight of childhood fancy – and imagined, after getting the ulcer, a filthy finger-nailed old woman fondling the sweets and then leaving them there, unattended. He pictured a fat child, who'd just had a crap and failed to wash his hands, fiddling at the sweets. People leave all sorts of germs on stuff. Very many do not wash their hands after using the loo. Some run the tap over their fingers, thinking this enough to remove germs – others only wash their hands after having a poo, but not after having a piss.... The things he notices while using public loos. He can't bring himself to dwell on the toilet habits and conditions of the medieval period without shuddering. But we're supposed to be wiser about such hygiene matters.

He looks around. Not many seated at the tables; couples sit in silence gazing at the television, occasionally one throws out a nugget of conversation that is met with a shrug, a glance away, a nod, a sentence or two.

What was this place back in 1983, and before?

He can't remember. Does. A cinema, yes … for years it was that. There'd been a balcony and occasionally he treated himself to a balcony seat, because on the lower floor he had once had chewing gum put in his hair. That bothered him: the not knowing if it had come his way like a stray bullet or if someone had singled him out. Smiles now when he recalls an intermission and looking across the aisle to see his girlfriend of two dates sitting beside a lad he knew – she'd stood him up. He had waited for half an hour past their appointed meeting time, and carried his hurt and disappointment to the pictures – thinking she had missed out on the surprise of a good show and a takeaway afterwards. Her name escapes him, and though he reaches deep into the corridors of his mind, it won't peep out from the dark – the name of the picture house does though, the Yellow Sky Cinema. And he remembers another thing, there had been a pub before the cinema and a barber's. The Castle Tavern and Carling's. On a roll, he thinks, but the young woman's name remains stubbornly elusive. It'll come to him later – when he stops trying too hard to remember. He had left before she became aware of his presence and went and consoled himself with a bag of chips, a cheeseburger and a cola – his first time to enter this chipper, his first time meeting Ena.

He enters the room an hour after Irene had declined his unspoken invitation to sit with him in the bar restaurant. The walk from the house back into town had been mostly in a brooding silence that sat like a strained wire between them. He'd tried to engage her in conversation, delivering some detail about a laneway where the mount of a ninth-century king, startled by a blacksmith busy at his forge, reared up and threw his rider to the ground, killing him. As though she cared. Why would she? This town and its history meant nothing to her. She won't be visiting again – and it's got nothing at all to do with the place, instead it's Dan and the horde of skeletons in his closet.

23

He beat his unfortunate wife. Broke skin, left her needing stitches, and begged his sister to furnish him with an alibi. My God. What sort of brute is he? To play on the fact that he had never raised his hand to her, as though she was in some way privileged, keeps her in a silent rage. Two weeks after the assault, his wife was dead. Murdered. Arrows point to him, of course. My husband.... What on earth have I married? A dormant monster? 'Look,' he says, irritated and unable to contain his own thoughts.

He's sitting on the edge of the armchair. She regards him coldly and makes for the bathroom, though she has no need to go.

'Irene,' he says, 'wait. Listen.'

She turns and says, 'I'm listening.'

He does that gesture with his hands, as if he's throwing every thought of his into the air.

'I have no defence, other than to say my head was in a bad place. I loved her and thought the world of her, and then I saw how she was never going to change. I think she married me to get away from her mother – and probably saw herself moving into my mam's house. Maybe that was her dream, to come from nothing to a little of something. But my mother didn't take to her and....'

'I don't care about her motives, or lack of, or anything like that. Whatever. Did you kill her?'

'No.'

'Did you do it by proxy?'

'Irene.'

'Tell me.'

'No, no, no.'

'Do you know who did?'

He shakes his head.

'The likely suspects?'

'A few – there would have been a few, yes, some I probably would know and others I wouldn't.'

'How did she die?'

He doesn't answer.

She says, 'Was she raped?'

A line deepens across his forehead. Wrinkles at the corners of his eyes enter into a huddle.

'No,' he says.'

His features, she thinks, have a look of surprise – as though he is hearing himself say this aloud for the first time.

'Raped?' she persisted, not really knowing why she was pushing for knowledge.

He says in a soft tone, 'No.'

'Something else?' she prompts.

'He didn't kill her outright – she'd a brain clot and it took over a day for her to die.'

'Suspects – surely there must have some leading candidates?'

'It could have been any one of five or six.'

'Give me their names. Write them down.'

'What, your cards will tell you who the killer is?'

'Dan, I'm not sure about us anymore. I'm not sure about you – so I have no idea if I'm going back with you on the same plane – that's a pure fact at this point in time. Maybe the cards might shed some light. I do get things right for my clients, at least occasionally – I do have repeat clients, you know. That should tell you something.'

'Irene – this is why I never told you. I knew you'd go off the rails.'

She gets to her feet. The room is cold. Touches the radiator – it's off.

'If you'd squared the past with me beforehand, right from the outset, then I don't know – yes – I could have done a runner – but you took that choice away from me. And you had no right to do that.'

'I never thought it'd come to this – not for a moment. My intention all along was not to come back here, so there was no need for me to risk losing you by spilling my guts. Last year, though, when I got sick, it set me to thinking. And I started to see her face, so clearly, in my dreams – after the operation. Till then, she was out of my mind. Not completely, how could she ever be, given the circumstances, but as close as. I started thinking about how she died, how people thought it was me who did it – some probably still do–'

Irene cuts in, 'Is Teresa one of those?'

He nods.

'Your own sister,' Irene says, 'who knows you.'

'What are you implying?'

'I'm not implying anything, really – did you ever hit your sister?'

The veins in his cheeks flame like overheated miniature pipes.

Irene frees a long sigh and holds her hand up in a stop sign.

'Once,' he admits, 'once....'

'Everything is once with you.'

'She used to hit my mother whenever she refused to sign a cheque out to her – she used to puck her in the arm. Mam used to be black and blue. I walked in one afternoon and caught Teresa in the act. Fucking sure I clocked her. I don't apologise for it. And I went to hit her again but I managed to check myself.'

'You couldn't manage to do likewise with poor Ena, no?'

'No,' he said, almost in a whisper.

'There were so many who could have done it. Luigi, she worked for him in the chipper. There was a lad called Benny, who was home from England at the time of the killing, another....'

24

Mirror Mickey didn't last too long in the job and then Luigi hired a succession of blokes. The thought occurred to me that he must have been hiring straight from the pages of *Weirdo's Weekly*, because they all looked like they'd been dragged screaming out of the gutter. In the end, he took on a woman called Han Kelly, an old one of fifty, who said she had nothing to do in the evenings and the job would suit her down to a tee. She used to work in a staff canteen at a factory. We got along, mostly.

Young Benny's wife had become a Friday-night regular. She was back from England. She was a pinched looking woman of maybe twenty-seven, pale-faced, and smelled of cheap musk perfume. Han knew her and if the counter was quiet they would talk about things, mostly about those who had recently died in the town. I never heard them discuss Young Benny. Han said one evening, after Young Benny's wife had left, 'Ena, do you know Beth?'

'Only to see.'

'That's enough – she wears no knickers. Keep that to yourself now.'

'How do you know?' I said, filling a bag of chips for a customer who'd said he'd be back in a minute to collect it.

Keep that to myself? Sure, who would I be telling?

'I just do,' she said, 'and such a temper – she would peel the hide off you if you gave her even a small reason. Like her father, she is.'

'Her husband used to work here,' I said, putting the bag into a brown paper one.

'So I heard. What was he like to work with?'

'Okay,' I said, watching the grease soak a patch in the bag.

'He stole on his nibs,' she said, checking the ketchup bottle for sauce.

'Yes.'

'Ah, sure, you've no luck for doing that sort of thing,' she said. 'What goes around, comes around.'

She liked to talk and to hear about what people were up to. She was eating into my shifts, though, getting one then two extra, and I thought about complaining to Luigi, but it dawned on me that they were having a fling, dancing to jukebox music late evening like I used do with Young Benny. The image of them together almost made me get sick into my first pair of high heels. And I wasn't too put out by the reduction in nights – I was getting tired of working late shifts and I enjoyed having some extra time off. I even went and played a little tennis in courts near the railway lines, but I couldn't take to the game. Took up again with old friends I'd told to get lost. Mammy said I should never hold a grudge – she, who had her hands full of grudges, said that.

I got my tattoo, it was mad looking, and Han said it was lovely, but why black, and I said, 'Why not?'

I washed my tattoo every day. Mammy said nothing after she saw it, and then when I asked her what she thought of it, she said, 'You didn't ask me for my thoughts before you got it, why bother asking for them now?'

'I might get in some petals, leading off from the stem,' I said, 'what do you think?'

She didn't answer, just shook her head. And rolled her eyes to the ceiling.

One evening, during the quiet part, Beth and this man, her father, came in. He was ruddy faced. He smiled. His black hair was slicked back, revealing a broad forehead with three small pockmarks ripe with blackheads. I used to think people wore their hair that way so there was less chance of it falling across their eyes and causing them to miss a beat of the day. He ordered a burger with no onions and a bag of chips without vinegar. Then he went to talking about a car with his daughter, saying she wasn't to buy it, because she'd be buying nothing only trouble. He spoke with authority, as if he knew what he was on about.

When Luigi came in, he frowned. I think part of him wanted to show them the door, but he wouldn't take what Young Benny did out on his wife. I wasn't even sure he would have done it, if he felt so inclined. He went into his office, closed the door, without saying 'God bless the work', which he always said upon his arrival. 'Good-looking young one,' her father said, when my back was to the serving counter. Saying it as if I wasn't there, shovelling his fucking chips into his mouth.

'You've got no taste, Dad,' Beth said.

I turned about and gave her a cutting look. He smiled at her. She was like her father in appearance, for sure, I thought. Reddish cheeks like the sun had gotten at them. Frustration ate into my skin, my insides, and wanted back out of them – I really wanted to say something to her and that creep she had for a father, but I was afraid. Afraid because of what Han had told me about Beth and her wicked temper, afraid because of her father's sinister look. I swallowed what I wanted to say. Fear added sauce to the words, making the taste all the more bitter.

I went with Hazel and Gilly to the pictures. The film was called *And Soon The Darkness*. It was about two young teachers cycling through the French countryside. They argue, go their separate ways, and one of them is murdered. Gilly said she'd love to be married to a foreigner, even a black man – she'd never seen one in real life. Hazel said she'd been to London when she was little and it was full of blacks – they were just real people, actually. She used that word 'actually' a lot.

I'd never seen a black man in real life. I couldn't see myself ever going out with one, unless I went to London – which I was thinking about doing. I thought my tattoo wouldn't look out of place there.

'Would you?' Gilly said, outside the cinema.

There was a lovely blood moon and bright stars, and I'd been admiring those and not zoned into the conversation.

'Would I what?' I said.

Hazel giggled and said, 'Let a black lad ride you?'

Gilly said, 'She'd let anyone ride her.'

I resented not so much what she said, more so the way she'd said it.

'Would I?' I said, wanting to hear her say it again, so I could feel justified for slapping her.

Hazel said, 'A bit mean, Gilly....'

'I was joking – I didn't – you know I was joking, right? God, I'm sorry, Ena.'

'I'm very fussy about who I give my favours to,' I said, quoting a line from a movie I liked.

'I've never ...' Hazel said, as we rounded the corner, just past the bakery.

'Me neither,' Gilly said, 'unless a finger is considered doing it.'

'Your own doesn't count,' Hazel reckoned.

'It was Sausage Brennan,' she said, her voice dropping.

'Jesus,' I said, with a measure of feigned disgust, 'him?'

'What about him?' Gilly said.

'Nothing,' I said, in a way that implied it was far from nothing.

'Tell me,' Gilly said, 'please.'

'He's just, you know, the ugliest boy in town, and he has the dirtiest fingernails.'

I was so glad to have gotten my revenge.

'I had drink on me,' Gilly said, 'a lot.'

I said nothing, which prompted Hazel to say, 'You … have you…?'

'A couple of times,' I said.

They stopped dead in their tracks. Wanted to know what it was like, if I was worried about getting pregnant, who was it with, did it hurt.

I wouldn't say the name, but I did after drinking a few cans of cider in Hazel's bedroom. Her parents stayed out late on Friday nights.

I'd been avoiding the girls for a while, since I told them they'd been using me to keep them going with treats of free food and drinks from Luigi's. This was their make-it-up-to-me night – according to Hazel.

'Him?' Hazel said, clasping Gilly's upper arm.

'Really?' Gilly said.

They made me feel like I'd had it off with Frankenstein, or worse.

'Him!' I confirmed.

'Were you drunk? You simply had to be out of it.'

I nodded the lie. You *bitch*, Gilly.

'That explains it so,' Gilly said.

'He's very old, isn't he?' Hazel remarked, passing round a bowl of red skin peanuts.

'Not that old,' I said.

'So, are you doing it with anyone now?' Gilly said.

'No, I got too much of a scare the last time – yeah – worrying about missing my period.'

'Rebecca is pregnant,' Gilly announced.

She was a girl from the class above ours. The same age, but she was really, really smart. We talked about her for a while and then we settled down to watch a video and drink some more cans. I stayed over, all three of us sharing the one double bed, and someone felt between my legs in the middle of the night – I never found out who, I was squashed between them. I quite liked it, so I just let her go ahead. I'm pretty sure it was Hazel. She couldn't meet my eye over the breakfast table.

Things kind of moved on after that night. Mammy was getting busier and busier and she kept saying I was out the door the moment I hit eighteen – I thought it was a joke – but it wasn't. She wanted Harry Freako Wolfe to move in but she wouldn't let him unless I was gone out of the house. Harry Wolfe would give shivers the creeps, but Mammy thought he was lovely.

She wanted an empty house, I'd gotten my siblings to safety, and I supposed it was high time to do the same for myself. I'd saved a little money and my wages were about enough to pay for a miserable bedsit above a pub. I went and looked it over but the rent was far too much. Tom Thumb would have found it too cramped. The sink taps leaked and the toilet looked like it had taken one shit too many. I told Mammy and she said I was a howl to be saying such things, that she would give me a few pounds for my birthday, to be getting on with things, because she didn't want Harry Wolfe being tempted by a young one living in the house – men are easily tempted, they let their willies point the way and follow it to their destruction.

We were getting along with each other, because she knew I was going.

I hadn't seen anyone I liked around town, and then one night a lad came into the chipper – I hadn't seen him before. He's nice, I thought....

25

She is in bed when he exits the bathroom. Her bedside lamp is off, his is on – warring dimly against the darkness. She lies on her side, hugging the edge of the bed. Usually she would be lying on her back, reading glasses on, with a biography or a spiritual book. Rarely does she read fiction – she says you couldn't make up some of the real life stories she has read. Other times she'd be lying awake thinking about a card reading that had gone great or badly – her cards, he had noticed, are spread on the coffee table.

'Are you awake?' he says.

She is, he believes, but he will have to wait until morning to learn of her thoughts.

Sleep evades him. Too many thoughts circle. He feels as though he has lost her and the notion wounds him. But he is not surprised – it had been going well between them and nothing in life runs too smoothly for too long. There is always a storm. This is another of theirs, and in the cold breaking light, he realises that in terms of their relationship it could prove a perfect storm. He does not want to lose her – anxiety at the prospect grips him – yet he had put things in motion that would drive them apart. The noose of his past has sent her running into the woods of her heart, away from him.

She stirs, eases from the bed. The wooden slats under the mattress groan at the release. He hears the opening and closing of the bathroom door. He gets up and dresses, ventures outside to the car park, and lights up a cigarette. Weather-wise, it's going to be a good day, he thinks.

The air is fresh, breezeless. Not many cars in the car park. Scrutinises the keep. That block of stone must have witnessed much in its five hundred years – how many souls have walked in its shadow? Ena had been thinking about renting a room there, after she left her mother's house – her mammy's, as she called it.

In the bedroom, she says, just as he is about to enter the bathroom, 'I have something to say.'

'Can it wait for a minute? I need to....'

'No. Right now, I want about 4,000 miles between us. But for now, I'm going to settle for much less. You're right. I shouldn't have come here. This is your history, yours to deal with. So, you do what you have to do around here. I'm going on vacation; I'm going to make the best of things.'

He's in pain from wanting to pee so badly, but he doesn't want to disappear behind the door in case she is gone when he emerges.

'Is that what your cards told you?' he says, bringing her eyes to the table.

'Yes.'

'I don't blame you, Irene. I had an idea this was all going to be messy, but ...' he shrugs.

'Is that the best you can do, say it's messy and shrug?'

'What do you want me to say? I was young, my wife was screwing around – sure I lost it. I shouldn't have but I did.'

Silence.

He turns and takes in a picture of a red sun on the rise above a lake fringed with rushes.

'Dan,' she says.

When she has his attention, she continues, 'I didn't ever imagine I'd end up living with a man suspected of murdering his wife – forgive me for allowing these little matters – these little previously unmentionables of yours, to preoccupy me. And you beat her ... I ...' she shakes her head.

'I–'

'Please. No, don't say it – don't say that you never laid a hand on me. I heard it all from Louis, yeah. For three years after he beat the crap out me, he swore he'd never do it again – but he did, he took a lot of my teeth when he did finally blow his gasket.'

'I'm not like him.'

He felt her eyes bore into his skull. 'In some ways you're so like Louis. You've got his hidden nature, that's for sure.'

'Irene....'

'Go piss,' she says, turning her back to him.

He finds himself unable to respond.

26

After she'd read about the Hill of Callan, some miles outside of Kildarragh, how it had once been home to the druidic high priest, Nuada, and a seat of learning for druids, she books a cab to pay the hill a visit. She gives the old balding guy a pick-up time before he leaves.

The hill broods, trees shade the trail, and the breeze is stiff. Callan isn't really a hill anymore, according to the cabbie – it's more like half a hill because its northern side has been quarried to a cliff face. He told her that modern druids conducted strange rituals on the hill at Halloween. The hill had been a fort of the Fianna, Ireland's Bronze Age special forces unit. Stay clear of the edge, the cabbie had added, the edge could creep up on you – several people had fallen to their deaths in recent years – no need to approach the edge, he'd repeated, warning signs all but hit you on the head.

Spot on there, she thought. I read the cards ... but I never copped the signs.

She reaches the top, stops at an old railed-off tower, scans about. Doesn't like the energy, the feel of the wooded hill. Maybe they're right to be obliterating it, she thinks, wishing she had pre-booked the cab for an earlier time.

Move on, give him space, give yourself that space, then see....

*

This train is for Galway. And that destination is as good as any. She buys a return ticket and sits on a bench at Platform 1. She'd skipped lunch in case he came after her and tried to persuade her to stay – if he'd done this, it would have been to lessen his guilt, to be able to say to himself that he had tried everything in his power to convince her to try and work things out – is it a case of work at the unworkable?

Of course, part of the problem is that the visit to Ireland has awakened some aspects of her own past. Incidents she'd forgotten about, far too unpleasant to remember. Incidents not far removed from Dan's own experiences. Maybe he's a little too much like Louis for comfort, but she is a little too much like his first wife for her comfort too....

27

I recognised him the same way you do strangers. You see someone around and you don't know his name or where he lives. He's there, like furniture you never much notice until it's gone or you trip over it or something.

I had dreams too. I wanted to have kids, a lovely husband and a nice home. Money wasn't important or fancy clothes or foreign holidays or eating out in posh restaurants. Shows you how naive I was – you can do nothing without money. Blind to the obvious, that was always my problem. Look at Mammy and her home of rags, and the terraced house we lived in, with the walls so thin you could hear the neighbours whispering to each other. I could hear them running up and down the stairs, pee in the bathroom. And Mr Byrne riding Mrs Byrne and the groans out of her and she telling him to go harder, you bollix. See her and him the next day and they'd be wearing pusses the length of a long run of shite. She'd be at Mass with the rosary beads dripping off her fingers and making these slow and deliberate signs of the cross in front of a statue of Jesus, as if He was only beginning to learn sign language.

And Dan's mother too – I used to see her, always three pews back from the altar and always sitting on the left, and keeping to the outer edge, not pushing in for anyone, turning her knees aside to let them pass. Most people would push along the seat, but I figured she had piles and they'd gotten nice, warm, and comfortable and she didn't want to go warming them up again further down the pew. Although she looked like a woman who wouldn't tolerate piles or them, her. Dan was occasionally there, his sister once; maybe it was their daddy's anniversary. She was the cutout of her mother. Upturned nose, small-eyed, which maybe stopped enough light ever getting in.

I had a dream too of being as good as they were, with their clothes and high opinions of themselves. Nice home, nice clothes and not having to worry about money.

'A bag of chips and a burger,' he said.

Han said, 'How's young Somers keeping this weather?'

'Fine, Mrs Kelly, and you?'

'Oh sure things could be worse – not much worse, mind you.'

I bagged the chips.

Han said, 'Here, Ena, do you know Dan?'

I glanced over my shoulder as I pressed down on his burger with the platter. 'No, hi.'

'Hi,' he said.

Han said, 'He lives down in that redbrick house on the Monasterevin Road, the big one.'

'There,' I said. 'Nice house.'

'Just saying,' Han said, 'because there are other Somers the far end of town – they're not cousins are they, Dan?'

'No.'

'I went to school with your mother.'

I turned his burger.

'How is she keeping? I mean after your dad died, God love him. A lovely man he was – a gent.'

'She's okay, thanks.'

'I heard she wasn't well.'

'She wasn't, but she is now.'

'Lost weight, though,' Han said.

I bagged his order, put it on the counter and gave him the price. He lingered at the jukebox and pushed in a coin. He chose 'Love Me, Love My Dog'.

Jesus.

When he was gone, Han said, 'His mother, God forgive me, is a right oul contrary so-and-so. She thinks her shite doesn't stink – you must know her – she wears stupid hats and is always talking to herself. She stands out a mile. Such a temper.'

Everyone Han tells me about, she says she has a temper.

'Oh,' I said, 'I think I do know her. I saw her a few times when I used to go to Mass.'

'Yes. Went funny in her loft after the husband died.'

A flood of customers off a tour bus came in, and she said, her voice going nice but false, 'Hello love, what can I get you?'

We were busy for an hour, followed by a lull, and then Beth and her father Owen came in. He wore a green short-sleeved T-shirt with the collar badly ironed, its ends turned up, like petals toward the sun. His face was far from being anywhere near warm. He'd a greasy head of hair, slicked back. Fingers thick as hammer handles, hairy-backed. One of his little fingers was missing – I wondered how he'd lost it.

He yapped away to Beth but was looking at me, never long enough to make me uncomfortable or for Beth or Han to think him rude. But it was a look that said much. God, I thought, what is it with men – I'm younger than his daughter – Jesus! Does he know or suspect that I was with Young Benny? His daughter's husband. No, if he did, surely he wouldn't find that a turn-on? For fuck's sake … men are not even a step up from the apes, not even a half step removed from retarded apes. That's what I think anyway. I hope he fucking chokes on his chips.

Now, he was speaking of Kildare town, some miles away, head turned to his daughter in her pretty red jacket, how he'd been rode out of money by a garage that had shut down overnight.

'I wouldn't go into that town again. I think more of myself than to grace its shadow with my presence.'

He chuckled at that.

Turning to me, he said, 'Don't put too much salt on those chips – you'll have me drinking barrels and as much I would like to, I haven't got the dough to do that.'

'England?' his daughter said, bringing up change from her pocket and putting it on the counter.

'Most likely,' he said. 'I've a few cars to service here for some old regulars and then I'll be off … it could be to that other England for me either.'

A jukebox song came on, playing Dr Hook's 'When You're in Love With A Beautiful Woman'.

I thought how the soul of that song was long gone, for it didn't affect me anymore to hear it being played; whereas before my heart would have wept at how Young Benny had codded me.

Then I felt the heat of Beth's stare on me and I tried not to turn as red as the ketchup, but I flushed purple under the burning of her eyes.

'I said would you hand me the vinegar?' she said. 'Are you awake? You're away with the fairies.'

'Sorry,' I said, and in handing over the vinegar bottle the tips of our fingers lightly touched.

Beth said, 'Give us a breast of chicken too.'

'Two breasts?' her father said with a leering smile.

'Cop on,' Beth said to him, sharp as.

After they'd left, Han said that when Owen had said England he'd meant either England or prison. Both had served time in prison: she for shoplifting and he for aggravated burglary. But that was all a long time ago – he was a good mechanic and people spoke highly of him in that regard. Not expensive either.

I stopped listening to her and was happy to see a couple of customers arrive in. Being busy kept my mind from bringing me to bad places and faces full of badness.

28

Her grave is neglected. Sunken, the wooden cross has long lost its varnished veneer and stands crooked. Grass, weeds, and a spray of grey pebbles carpet the length of Ena's stretch. He studies the names on the very fancy headstones either side of her. Names and addresses in stark bold, as though it matters who they were and where they had lived and not how. She is dead for longer than she had been alive. This happens to us all….

We will all be ancestors one day, he remembers his mother saying.

Magpies create a racket in the tall pines that run the length of the boundary wall. The sky to the east is turning a washed-out lavender. It had taken him some time to locate the grave. A lot had gone to their maker in thirty-one years and the names of some on the headstones had thrown faces at him – people he hadn't thought of in years. There is nothing like a graveyard for washing your soul in a frozen pond.

Does he lie here, too? The man or men who killed her? Is he buried in a respectable plot, with ornate granite and grave decorations? Etched words like 'Sadly Missed', 'In Loving Memory', and so on?

Or is he still breathing?

He has brought a bunch of lilies for his dead wife, and places them at the base of the wooden cross.

He tries to right the cross but it refuses to budge – it is as though she will not allow him to do even that much for her. Memories come like the first snowflakes of a blizzard: slowly, hesitantly, growing stronger, more numerous, in no arranged pattern.

'Ena …' he says, her name tight in his throat.

29

Irene gets off the train at Athlone and waits for her connection to Galway. A young woman someway along the platform appears to shrink under the weight of her boyfriend's arm. She passes them, catching a faint whiff of the young man's cologne.

The waiting room is almost empty. Partial to ginger cake, she orders two slices and a latte from a woman at the tiny shop in the corner, and brings them to a chair. She picks at her cake – it is too dry and the coffee too weak. Ordinarily, she would complain, but this is Ireland and from what she herself has seen and heard from Dan, the Irish complained but certainly not long or loudly enough.

She forces herself to eat one of the slices – reproaching herself for not choosing a sandwich – and bins the remainder, even the latte, which had been an exercise in drinking a paper cup of hot tastelessness.

She turns her spectacles thoughtfully, thinking on how Dan had flinched at her words. What did he expect? For her to demur, to behave as though none of what he had done actually mattered in the scheme of their lives?

Her anger is a ball of fire in her stomach. She dismisses Dan from her mind and turns her thoughts to her father. He is a long time gone from this world.

Sometimes, his face springs to her mind and she feels the loss of him acutely. A funny man, he was always more generous than he could afford to be. Would she have turned out a different person if he had lived even into her early teens? Would he have kept Mama in check? On their wedding anniversary, her mama's face was so full of sorrow that she'd tried to wash away with a smile she had dug up from somewhere. She gave up, lost heart, went bad, because being bad diluted and numbed the memories.

Back on the train, she watches cloud rolling over a mountain ridge, unfurling towards the fields. Afternoon drizzle flecks the window as the train pulls into the station at Galway. She finds, after about an hour, a B&B down a narrow lane. Yellow pebbledash, freshly painted white sills and varnished door does not prepare her for the state of the room.

Her bathroom is so dirty that she wouldn't use it for fear of contagion. So filthy that her skin crawls. And the middle-aged proprietor, Valerie, is so charming she disarms her of the caustic remarks that sit on the edge of her tongue. How on earth does she live like this? Her own living quarters could hardly be any better – Irene instinctively knows that they are not. It is all she can do not to crack up with laughter when Valerie tells her over tea that she had a big clean-up a few days before she arrived, seeing as there are some other guests coming – she'd taken the overload from the guesthouse next door – and some people could be right fusspots.

'I knew by looking at you that you weren't like them. You have a down-to-earth quality about you....'

'Ah ...' Irene says, smiling.

'Will you be here for dinner?' Valerie asks.

'I'm meeting somebody later,' Irene lies.

Heck, can the woman talk.

Valerie wears brightly coloured clothes and to make an extra income she designs and fashions knitwear for the tourist trade.

'I must show you,' Valerie says.

'Please – tomorrow, Valerie, if you don't mind?'

The tip of Valerie's nose has a red spot.

Oddly enough, Dan gets them in the same place.

After dinner, she finds a pub Valerie recommended. The recess lights shine like small suns on the black-speckled countertop. A chap with an off-centre nose, another with a wedding ring cut into the fat of his finger, discuss the musician who has just taken a break from the stage. On the walls there are turn-of-the-century photographs of the owner's ancestors, a time when the pub traded as a hardware store.

She reels out what she had said to Dan after she had come back from the Hill of Callan to find him watching John Denver on Sky Arts, singing 'Some Days Are Diamonds'. His eyes were moist and he did not blink the tears away. She heard a few of the words. It was a song about lost love. Anger rippled through her – what the hell was the matter with him? Goddamn it, the woman was years dead and there he was, in a time warp, letting a sad song bring her back to him.

'Know what that's like,' she spat, 'seeing you there – it's like you're telling me that she was the last time you saw and knew true happiness.'

'I'm going to find the killer,' he'd said. 'I have to, you know … then, I'm going to fix things with you.'

'Yeah,' she said. 'I'm outta here.'

'Irene.'

'Go fuck yourself … hon.'

Irene orders a double vodka, she who hasn't touched the hard stuff in three years. This is what he has done to her.

30

The flap of the letterbox closed with the sound of a face slapped. It was stocktaking and cleaning morning. Luigi had gotten wind of a health inspection. In the dusty light pouring in through the top window, I could see patches of dirt on the tiled floor I hadn't noticed under artificial light. God, the smell. The cold greasy atmosphere brought goose pimples to my forearms.

After that morning – and we cleaned like crazy, myself and Han – I began to hate Luigi's. Hated the idea of going in there, hated being in there. That's what sunlight cast on stuff did for me, made me hate.

'Fliers,' Luigi said, waving them, 'and bills. Pain in the hole.'

He went into his office and shut the door.

Han nudged me with her elbow, 'I caught him in there the other day, bawling his eyes out.'

'Are things really that bad?' I said.

Han crinkled her nose, scratched her cheek. She wore a blue nylon work coat stained with ketchup and oil spatter. She had had her hair done and it smelled of lacquer – her hair was thinning and if she didn't wash it every day you could see the bald patch shine through.

'If's he crying, it must be pretty bad. I didn't see him shed a tear when his brother Gino died – God, he was a lovely man, that Gino.'

'Money?'

'More than that, if you ask me.'

I was glad when lunchtime came and I could get out of the cave. I hadn't to work that evening. Han said she would try to worm the problem out of him after they'd closed up. If the takings were good, he might be in the mood for talking. She suspected his business was close to folding and believed we had a right to know. The morning mists of the hills were in her eyes, and I understood she was terrified of being made redundant – the last thing she wanted was to sit at home and stare at the four walls and a telly. She confided in me she'd once come close to slitting her wrists during an episode of *Star Trek*. She loved Captain Kirk – her late husband used to look like him. She would, she promised, bring in a photograph to show me. Never did.

Outside, the wind sang silent words of misery. I always felt the cold more than most. Mammy said I was like Aunty Babs, who was always cold on the hottest of days. I was about to cross the road when I heard him say, 'It's a cold one – even with the sun shining, yeah?'

It was the nice guy who'd come in a week or so ago.

'Yeah,' I said.

He chewed gum. I could tell he was nervous. He was skinny, wore blue jeans and black Gola trainers.

His brown hair hung just below his ears and smelt of coconut shampoo. We crossed the road together. I cross roads quickly, looking both ways. I don't think I ever told him why. Or maybe I did, I'm not sure.

Leading up, he was, to asking me out, and I think he went to a couple of times, but his lips froze. At the corner of the bakery, he said, 'Would you like to come out on a date with me?'

He expected me to refuse and that nudged me into saying, 'Yeah, okay – why not?'

'The pictures?'

I pulled a face, 'There's nothing much good on.'

'I was thinking of going to Newbridge.'

Five miles away. I'd never been to that picture house.

'They're showing a re-run of *Saturday Night Fever*.' he said, as if it was a trump card or something.

'Bee Gees?' I said, 'nah.'

His face looked like I'd let the air out of it.

'But I heard it's good,' I said, 'so, okay....'

'Great,' he said, 'there's a disco on—'

'At the convent hall, I know.'

'We could go there....'

'Pushing your luck, aren't you?'

'No.'

'I'll see you down at the hop tonight, and we can get to the pictures together another night.'

'Great.'

'Do you have a car?'

'No, not yet,' he said, 'but I will in a short while. Soon as I pass my driving test. My mother has a good mechanic and he's keeping his eye out for something reliable. The thing is, he's hard to get – when work is slack he legs it England.

He scanned my expression for signs of disapproval and disappointment. I didn't care what he had or hadn't – I was making small talk and trying to keep my nervousness from showing.

'I was thinking we could take an early bus over,' he said, 'maybe Friday.'

'Okay,' I said.

I had to do a re-think in a flash – was I working? No.

'Is that all right?' he said, alarmed, possibly thinking I had a clash of dates, which was no bad thing for him to think.

After we'd parted, I don't know, I walked with a bounce in my step. He was my first real date. Young Benny was different. I didn't like his face coming into my mind or what we'd done in his flat. Thinking of him didn't unduly bother me – but whenever I thought of him, his mother came along too. Funny though, that the memory of his mother hadn't put me off going with him – but then I had no issue with his mother but with what had happened to her. No one deserved to die the way she did.

Mammy was in a shitty mood when I got home. She was in the sitting room, legs crossed. I could hear the kids playing football on the green. The language from them was something terrible. The telly wasn't on. She was looking at herself in the green screen, looking at herself, the blinds, and the blue and grey sky.

'Is something the matter?' I said.

She folded her arms. Stared me out of it.

'I want it back,' she said.

'Want what back?'

'Don't!' she said, wagging her forefinger.

'Mammy – I haven't got a clue what you're on about.'

'I had four hundred quid saved – it's gone – I checked an hour ago and the chest is empty.'

I shook my head and said, 'I swear to God, it wasn't me – it wasn't.'

'There's only the two of us living here.'

True, but people were coming in and out all the time. Customers, that Wolfe lad.

'It wasn't me,' I insisted.

'Well, who was it then?'

'How would I know?'

I could tell she really believed in her heart I was to blame.

'Going on your previous form,' she said.

'What?' I said, absolutely bewildered.

It lit on me. Luigi's ... she hadn't believed me when I said I'd nothing to do with that theft.

'And you diddled people out of their change too. I tell you, it all comes out in the end – the truth.'

'Mammy – Jesus....'

'If you leave the money back....'

'I didn't even know where you'd hid it.'

I couldn't prevent the tears forming. Hurt, angry. Swirling in my guts. Jesus, that Mrs Foster and her fucking son really messed with my head. Mammy was making me feel that I was guilty.

'You don't believe me, not a word, do you?' I said.

'No,' she said.

'I'll go then, Mammy, is that what you want? Is it?'

'It might be a good idea. Wasn't that your plan anyway?'

Not this soon, I thought.

'Well I'm not staying here,' I said, leaving her with a hanging gob.

I grabbed a holdall and stuffed my clothes into it. I'd no idea where I was going, where I would spend the night. I couldn't go to my aunts. Mammy would have had them tipped off, and besides, everyone, siblings included, had become strangers.

So I took a bedsit, sat on the bed, and cried for hours.

31

'Yes, cemeteries do scare me,' he whispers.

At the time Ena was interred, there were no graves beside or in front of her   now there are rows and rows of them running in all directions.

Ena had a sister and a brother. Did they ever come here? Obviously not, or hadn't in a long while. Her mother, he had heard, moved to England shortly after Ena's murder. His parents are buried here too. Their plot needs some minor work, weeding mainly, a washing of mildew from the granite headstone, perhaps a fresh layer of pebbles. Ages, so many different ages – he found it all so depressing and yet paradoxically, he'd thought it uplifting in another way: no matter what shit came your way, there was an end to its flow. When life and people weighted you down, you just needed to remember the road marker – that's all you had to do.

Remember.

'But we forget,' he whispers, 'constantly.'

He pauses at a grave marker older than the ones he had passed – blotched with white lichen, and decides to make a call. He isn't going to allow her to continue sleeping in a grave that is about as close to anonymity as one can get – in a hundred years or whatever, it would be okay for her name to be washed off and be a sad marker with the lettering long gone, to announce the presence thereunder of anonymous bones – a mere catalogue number if ever the object of an archaeological dig.

'I doubt if I'll be back this way again, Ena….'

He tells her about Irene, their blow-up, his close call that he fears is just a hint at how things will pan out for him.

'And I have this fear, Ena, that's there's nothing – nothing at all on the far side. If there was, wouldn't you have found a way to let me know who it was? That's where it all unravels for me … religion … at the end of the day we only have what people tell us, yeah?

'And … I don't know. If God exists, I'm here – I want to see Him, hear Him … and believe me I've invited Him. But He never shows up … if you can't tell me, then I used to hope that maybe He would – I want to know who put you in the ground, Ena. Why is that such a big ask?

Is there anyone dead who is listening?'

32

In the morning, her thoughts swim hard to the surface. Opens her eyes. Morning light seeps in between a gap in the brown curtains. Irene raises her head a fraction from the pillow and stares at the back of the woman's head. A mass of dyed black. The air stinks from stale alcohol. Irene lowers her head gently to the pillow. Her head is pounding. She looks under the duvet. Fully dressed. Thank Jesus. Is she, this other person? Pinches the duvet and lifts it.

Yes, thank God.

It turns out the woman is Valerie, her B&B lady.

'You were in a fierce bad way last night,' Valerie says in her kitchen.

It was her bedroom in which Irene had awakened.

'When did you come on the scene?' Irene asks, nursing her coffee.

'Too late – you were passed out, your head lying on the counter – I went in there by chance, so the angels were looking down on you.'

'Thanks,' Irene says.

'You shouldn't be touching the drink, but I think you already know that,' Valerie says.

Her complexion is glossy with moisturiser. Her nose short and thin, with narrow nostrils that flare a little before she speaks.

'I don't usually – I used to lean quite heavily on the juice, but….'

'You get the occasional trigger?'

'A-ha.'

'I put you in my bed because I was afraid that you might choke to death – it happened to a friend of mine years ago. You never forget stuff like that – at least, I don't.'

Irene wants to open up and say she's been feeling depressed lately. It's as if the clouds that used to be grey have turned black, and with the change of colour, there has come an added weight. But she understands this is part of her, her depression – if that's what it is, it might be the wrong name – has got to do with Dan and his history, his lies, his withholding of truths, and she does not want uncertainty in her life. Not now, at her age. She wants security, good ground. Before the revelations she had been in a relationship she thought was boringly stable, overly predictable … which was not what she wanted either.

The urge to up and leave Dan was ripe in her up until the time he fell ill. She wouldn't walk out on him when he was in bad shape. His cancer had taken her mind and heart away from hitting another Greyhound bus.

'Well,' Valerie says, 'you have to be mindful of cirrhosis of the liver – it's killed three of my friends in the last year, you know, one of them was a closet drinker – how she kept that a secret for years escapes me.'

'Thanks for everything, Valerie.'

She becomes certain of one thing – it had finally hit home – she needed to leave Dan for good. It's as if someone has taken a crowbar to her heart and stuffed a sack of truths inside.

She winces at a sudden jab in her ribs. It passes.

'Are you okay?' Valerie asks.

'Fine. My stomach feels like the inside of the hotel's slop barrel.'

'I've got something for that.'

She'd intended to stay a while longer, but she has an itch to travel, and makes her way to Lahinch and the Cliffs of Moher. She may as well see as much as possible, because she will not be setting foot in Ireland again. She has made up her mind to tell Dan they are done.

33

I slept late and wanted to get back into bed about ten minutes after I'd gotten out. Old and faded green carpet covered the floor, whiskers of it ran up the off-white skirting board. The bathroom was tiny, the grout had turned black between the white shower tiles; there was no shower curtain. No toilet seat and the cistern was high against the ceiling, with a chain to tug on. But at least, I suppose, staring out through the window onto the street, there weren't clothes lying everywhere and strangers shuffling in out and out. I could manage. I would manage. Mam had rightly pointed out to me that I was leaving home anyway – true – but I didn't want to leave with bad feelings staining the air between us. I got to thinking that leaving with bad blood was Mammy's way of handling the guilt at letting me go. My going had to be my decision, not hers; perhaps she couldn't even handle a joint decision. The stolen money was just a convenient smokescreen. She wanted me out and Freakie Wolfe in.

At least now I didn't have to linger on in school. Maybe Luigi might give me an extra shift or maybe I could waitress somewhere part-time. Whispers mushroom, and some here are always eager to believe the worst they get to hear about a person. Jesus, I would be well set if I'd robbed as much as what I was accused of stealing.

I called down to the chipper and knocked on the door. Luigi didn't usually open up until midday and it was almost that time. Han let me in. She walked ahead of me. A vein like a purple snake ran down her plump calf. It must pain her a lot. At her age, she shouldn't have to be on her feet as much – she'd told me she couldn't hack spending the evenings alone. This was only partly true, I thought; three quarters of the truth was that she had to work out of sheer necessity. I felt for her and silently hoped I would never end up in a similar situation.

Han moved around to the serving side of the counter. The radio was on. She'd been drinking a mug of tea and eating a Jaffa biscuit and went back to doing that. I guessed she wasn't in the mood for talking. I wondered if Mammy had had a word in her ear.

'Are you okay, Han?' I said.

I began to think along the lines that she'd heard bad news from Luigi about the chipper. If that was the case, though, she'd have said it right off, at the door.

'It's my leg, it's giving me a tonne of grief,' she said 'What brings you in on your day off?'

'Is Luigi in?'

'He is. What do you want him for?'

Nosey cow.

If Luigi gave me extra shifts it could mean her losing some – but I would be taking back those that used to be mine in the first place. Still....

'To see if he'll give me my wages in advance – I'd to move out of Mammy's in a hurry.'

'Jesus, what happened there, love?'

Suddenly she was alive, as if she'd gotten a charge of energy.

'Ah, the usual. Over nothing.'

The feeling came to me that I shouldn't confide a whole lot in Han, and this came with a pinch of sadness, because up to that point I would have told her anything without checking myself. I recalled something she'd told me not long after she'd started working here: 'People turn themselves like you'd turn a mattress. Trust no one, m'dear.'

I thought, of course, she'd excluded herself.

Luigi's fat fingers were dancing on his calculator. Reams of paper on his desk, half a cod on a paper bag. A film of sweat across his hairline. His nose had blackheads and I asked myself how he didn't notice them in the mirror as he shaved. They were huge.

'Don't ask for a raise,' he said, smiling.

'No. But ... pay in advance,' I said, going on to explain my new accommodation arrangements.

He rubbed his hands together, leaned back in his chair, and said, 'Okay.'

Such relief. I was over the moon that he hadn't made a song and dance about it. I didn't mention the extra shifts. I just couldn't bring myself to do that – I wouldn't have been able to look Han in the eye. Though I realised what I had gone into Luigi's office to do, she had done weeks earlier and hadn't given any consideration toward my feelings or circumstances. She probably saw me as a young mindless thing, working for pocket money and not to put a loaf in my mouth.

'Do you want some advice, Ena?' he said, after he'd paid me straight from his wallet. A bulging black-leather wallet.

'Okay,' I said.

'Do your Leaving Cert, get a career – take the opportunity to educate yourself. This sort of work isn't going to buy you the nice things in life – not even the basics, probably.'

'Thanks.'

'Do you want some more advice?'

I said nothing, because I wasn't sure if I liked how his face had changed – it had become sly.

I felt uncomfortable and expected he was about to say something inappropriate. If he had, and I believe he was about to until he read the concern in my expression, it was most likely that I would have vomited over his nest of blackheads.

'Emigrate,' he said, going back to his calculator.

34

Sooner than face into being alone in his room at the B&B and also wanting a change from the fare on offer at the pub, he walks to the retail village, where he enters an Italian restaurant and orders a vegetarian lasagne and a glass of house red. His feet are sore after the walk from the cemetery; his middle toe in particular gives him trouble.

He'd waited at the cemetery to meet the man who would inscribe Ena's details on her headstone. The stonesmith, Adam, wasn't from the locality and knew nothing of her story.

He had done graves, he'd said, for a couple of murder victims. Men – a Pole and a Brazilian jockey. And this week there'd been a couple of suicides and a road fatality. The strangest request he'd ever had was to erect a headstone with a living man's name on it – the guy had a terminal illness and wanted to leave everything organised for his wife. He'd been given six weeks to live, but two years on, he's still alive....
'His wife's name had to be added to the headstone because she took a heartie.'

Dan assumed he'd meant a heart attack.

'No one's guaranteed his next breath,' Adam lamented.

It begins to drizzle. Fall is in the air. There is that stillness, of the earth holding its breath, the beginning of change in the colouring of the trees. He thinks to ring Irene but is uncertain if she will answer and defers the decision until after his meal. She, after all, might contact him.

She is the one who walked, so perhaps the ball is in her court. Irene is as a stubborn as he is; giving ground and reaching compromise has always proven difficult.

Ring? No.

Maybe later. Emergency contact only, she'd written on the note.

Positive?

The drizzle has moved up a gear into hard rain. It is down for the rest of the day, he is sure, and he has not brought a jacket. There's a North Face shop across the way from the restaurant – he would treat himself to a light rain jacket.

There is a call. His heart gives a small dance of joy but it is not her – it is Adam with his quotation and a date for carrying out the works. Acceptable, if a little overpriced, he senses.

He has to pay above the going rate in order to jump the queue.

In the shop, he buys a navy jacket and a grey woollen hat. Standing outside, on the street corner, he calls Irene.

He is about to hang up when she says, 'Hello?'

'Hi, Irene?' he says, 'can we talk … please? Just talk?'

Silence.

He can, he is sure, almost hear her thoughts turning over.

'Your number came up as unknown,' she says.

35

She is enjoying – if that is the right word – the break from him. There is no walking on eggshells, no brooding atmosphere with which to contend – except for her own.

The rain has arrived, blown in from the Atlantic. Her room has a view of the ocean and with the window open she can smell the salt air, see the surfers ride in to shore on the high waves. If the rain clears, she'll walk along the pier to clear her head. During the bus journey to Lahinch, she made the decision to to fly home from Shannon Airport – she plans to be packed and gone from the house before Dan gets back to the States. Briefly, she'd considered forgiving him and moving on. But his past is blacker than black and that's a colour that sticks. She knew she would never manage to wrap her head around his deceit. And he expects me to understand that he'd a good reason for hammering his first wife. Circling her mind like a great white shark is her suspicion that he possibly killed Ena too. Already, he has hidden far too much. He might be shielding his crime – and only God knows what else besides.

She will tell him, of course, after she's left the house. Financially, she has enough savings to set up home – maybe somewhere small in the next town over five miles away, as she doesn't want to lose her client base.

At the table in her bedroom, she does something she very rarely does – she deals herself a hand of cards.

36

He was waiting for me at the bus stop. He smiled and I smiled back. I was half-expecting him not to show, and half-hoping he wouldn't. I'd wanted to scrub the bedsit from top to bottom and put new linen on the bed – there was none, just a bare blue mattress with a duvet covering it. Dan wore a new pair of Wrangler jeans, a red and black lumber jacket. He'd washed his hair and shaven the few thin whiskers he'd had on his chin. I couldn't fault him for trying. He was nice, though. I tried to compare him to some film star – he slightly resembled one – but I couldn't think of his name; he wasn't very famous or very good looking either.

The bus was late. We stood inside the bus shelter, not saying anything because there were people standing close-by. When the bus came, he let me go ahead of him to find seats while he paid for the tickets. I sat in at the window, waved at Han who was on her way into work, but she didn't see me.

'So,' he said when he joined me, 'how was your day?'

'Fine. Yours?'

'I'm glad to be getting my head out of the books.'

'You're doing the Leaving?'

'Repeating it,' he said. 'I didn't get the points I needed last year to get the course I wanted.'

'What are you planning to do?'

'Dunno really. An accountant, administration …
something along that line. You?'

'A nurse,' she said.

It was the first thing that came into my mind. He was
nearly a year younger than me. Had to be bright, because he
had sat his first exams very young.

'You're doing the exam this year too?' he said.

She took in his hands. His fingernails were spotless,
perfectly curved. Young Benny's had been bitten to the
quick. I'll say this much for his mother, she brought him
up to keep himself clean. Unlike Young Benny, he wouldn't
dream of stepping off the path and say he was going for a
slash, or emerge from the toilet after dropping a number
two without washing his hands and then try to finger her.

'I'm supposed to be,' she said, deciding it was probably
better not to dig a hole for herself. 'I'd like to become a
nurse, but….'

'It must be tough trying to find time to study and work
in Luigi's,' he said.

'Yeah, it is.'

'I–'

'Can I ask you a question – do you mind?'

'No, not at all.'

'Do I smell like the chip shop?'

'No,' he smiled, 'you don't.'

37

This morning, his age comes at him like a belt from a hammer. He had not slept very well. His stomach feels unsettled, as though someone had squeezed his heart and the juice had seeped....

He climbs out of bed, rubs his eyes. Irene isn't coming back. Not here, or anywhere else where he draws oxygen. She left no luggage behind. The sole item in the room belonging to her is a hairbrush. It holds a couple of strands of her hair – the sum of their time together.

He boils the small blue kettle to make coffee and has to settle for tea because the tray is out of coffee sachets.

Nights are the worse for dealing with situations of loss. At least it has always been so for him.

He didn't sleep a night through for six months after his father died, and the same with his Mam. Ena, too. Memories, the forgotten ones, would sieve through the darkness and pierce.

She died carrying his surname, yet they were not married in the true meaning of the word. He wonders how many people actually are. In their case, he supposes, they were sometimes married – whenever she decided to return from her wanderings to share their flat. He wasn't enough for her. Perhaps if he'd been stronger that first time he'd found out about her cheating, and gave her her marching orders, things might have panned out differently. He loved her and he would have forgiven her anything – sure, he sulked, sure, he got mad with her and whoever, and sure, there were times when he swore he'd washed his hands of her forever. But the iron in his veins never stayed hot. The love in his heart for her did.

Strange, he thinks, he would not display such patience and forgiveness with Irene. Has that to do with maturity or the fact that he had only ever really loved one woman in his entire life?

Thirty-one years … it's a long time to be dead. How would he feel if Ena had lived? Where would he be? Would he have come home – to Ireland – to see her? Hardly.

It's a question he asks of the mirror as he takes a blade to his chin. Perhaps he would not have gone to America; they might have had a child or two; she might have changed or he could have and they might have gone their separate ways and his love for her would have faded. Conjecture! Stop! The facts are these: when she died, he was in love with her.

She was going to change, she told him.

'I swear I'm going to quit drinking, and get a proper job. Okay? I promise. Dan?'

That was after he'd beaten her … she'd come to him and in a dramatic way, apologised to him for pushing him over the edge…. He'd expected a warning, to be berated, threatened not to ever lay a finger on her again, unless he wanted to be swallowing his balls. Instead, he got offerings of tears and genuine remorse, and for two weeks she didn't take a drink. She cooked dinners, cleaned their miserable little flat. Then one night she didn't come home…. Based on experiences with her, he believed she had fallen off the rails again.

Convinced of this, he wasn't worried about her safety. Far from it: he was in a deep and dark place – in a temper he contained between his flesh and bones. It was all he could do not to search for her and give her a dose of what would bring her back to him. Remorse at what he had previously done, a sickening strain of guilt, restrained him.

He rinses his face. Looks at the mirror and says, 'You could easily have killed her – someone else did that for you … and people thought it made you happy for it to be done.'

A woman can drive a man to hit her – she can plan for it to happen.

Did Ena, plan?

No. She was just being the person she turned into.

Now, after all this time, you want to do what – to find her killer?

I would love to know.

You have an idea, though – don't you?

A suspicion.

Who cares – after all this time? Not her mother, brother and sister? Who?

Her family think I killed her.

His thoughts spin.

No – other people did at the time – friends too – both mine and hers. Her brother, sister, aunts … her mother didn't. She knew by me I hadn't harmed her.

Intuition guided them?

Yes. Perhaps.

She didn't know, you'd given her daughter a terrible hiding, did she?

Not at the time. The guards told her. But she still didn't believe I'd killed Ena.

No. Why is that?

Perhaps she knows who did.

Your mother? Did she think you killed....

I....

Did she?

She said she knew I hadn't. That it wasn't in me.

38

The young woman in front of Irene has a tattoo on the back of her neck. 'Unbreakable.'

She smiles and wonders what had tested her so much to prompt that word into ink.

Irene had been thinking of having one done, a lace of red roses around her ankle. A butterfly above it. Perhaps she would. Why not?

Dan told her that his Ena had a black rose tattooed on her ankle, and he never liked it. It seemed to be a leak of the darkness she'd carried within her.

She moves her tray along the serving rail and asks the chef for white pudding, fried eggs and sausages. Sits to a window seat, her back to the wall: she hates having a blinkered view of what's around her. He hadn't called her again – she thought he might – didn't leave her a voice message either or send a text.

He isn't going to fight for her.

And it's not because he is aware that she is a lost cause. At any rate, it isn't something she'd expected to happen. They'd been more companions than lovers in their marriage. A relationship built on each other's need to banish loneliness – they got along, overlooking the fact that there was minimum passion between them. They'd each accepted less because less was much more than they already had.

Back to square one, she thought, but right now, it looked a more attractive proposition. Yet, she had to speak with him about something.

A message had been gleaned from her cards.

39

John Travolta. Now, he could dance. The music, the songs, the dancing, oh, I loved it. There aren't many films I would watch over and over, but *Saturday Night Fever*.... It made me feel light and happy inside. It was as though someone had cast light on my soul.

Condoms, rubbers – I'd never used one, and to hear John Travolta talk about them was enlightening – I felt Dan shift in his seat during those scenes. He was shy. He didn't put his arm around me or his hand on my breast. I wouldn't have slapped him if he did, I'd just have taken it away gently and scolded him with a look. If he'd persisted, I might have let him.

Dan said he'd enjoyed the film, but I doubted if he did. I think he said things just to agree with me, pushing his own thoughts aside, making out that they weren't as valuable as mine.

We didn't sit in the back row as I thought we might, but he was hesitant about leading the way and instead we found seats midway down, guided by the usher's torchlight. A classier cinema than the one in Kildarragh.

'Better breed of flea,' Dan said, which I thought funny.

During the interval, he bought cola and popcorn, although I had said I wasn't hungry. I went to the loo and had a ciggie outside, just to calm my nerves. Then I chewed on spearmint gum to replace the tobacco smell in my mouth.

After the film, it was about ten-ish, and we'd an hour and a bit to wait for the last bus home. He asked if I wanted a bag of chips and a burger. I thought he was winding me up, but he wasn't – I could tell by his blank expression that he genuinely thought I'd love nothing better than to eat takeaway grub on my night off. I said no.

Actually, I was starving, but I hadn't wanted to come across as one of those girls who would fleece a fella. Gilly and Hazel could be that way inclined and milk a boy they knew they wouldn't be dating again. I did think it was a sign of how thoughtless Dan could be at times.

He should have been more in tune with how I would feel about that question.

A full yellow moon gazed down on us as we waited for the late bus to take us home. I think we were nervous and that nervousness showed in long silences that we took turns in trying to smother.

'I'd say they'll make a sequel,' he said, hands in his pocket, small puffs of vapour coming from his mouth.

'Definitely,' I said, not knowing what else to say.

He wasn't one of the girls, so I couldn't tell him that I thought John Travolta had a lovely arse and that he melted my knickers. Girls would screech laughing at that remark – we wouldn't mean it really – or maybe we would – it'd be said for the laugh – meaning it or not didn't matter. I could have said it to Young Benny; he wouldn't have been jealous. But I think that would have been because he didn't care about who did what to me.

We stood close to each other. I studied the style of the girls passing us by on the street, and thought how I'd love to have some pretty clothes. My wardrobe consisted of three pairs of jeans, two pairs of shoes, some blouses and T-shirts and a sweater. A rain jacket. I had nothing for good wear – it had bothered me before the date but I pushed it to the back of my mind. Everything he had on was new or newish, right down to his brown leather shoes.

These were highly polished – the smell wafted right up from them. I thought only old guys polished their shoes. Later, I would think that was half of Dan's problem: he was an old guy before his time. I had loads of little accessories and these sort of glossed my appearance up a little, or so I liked to think. Cheap things, like you'd put in a home to make it look warm, lived-in and liveable in.

I picked up that he was bursting to ask me out again. I wasn't pushed whether or not he managed to get the words out. I felt like I needed some time to digest the evening, to make up my mind about him. The disco had been okay – he danced like he'd a poker up his hole, shoulders raised. He was so out of his comfort zone.

He squeezed my hand on the bus and asked if I'd like to go out with him again. I said yes, but only because I didn't want to hurt him and hadn't made up my mind – a second date would probably tell me more about him.

He wanted to walk me home and I had to insist strongly that I was fine. He thought I lived with Mammy. In the end, to shut him up, I agreed to let him walk me to the top of the estate. He said over and over that it wasn't safe for a young woman to be out on her own this time of night. I began to think Dan had never done anything wild or off-the-cuff in his life.

Sometimes, if I got a notion, I would just run with it, without thinking it through. Impulsive, Mammy said of me, using that word to say robbing stuff wasn't really my fault. An impulsive streak Daddy passed on to me.

He kissed me on the cheek, turned, and walked away, up the road, past the petrol station. I turned full about and went back uptown.

I'd a separate key to a black door right next to the pub. The pub should have been closed but I heard a ballad being sung in there. When an old fella came out, he held the door open for me – I'd been rooting for the key to the black door.

'He's calling for the last round – you might be lucky.'

I went in, because I was hungry and thought I might buy two packets of King crisps – I liked that brand – and a bottle of cola with ice and a slice of lemon. Habits have small beginnings.

40

Thus far, he has not met anyone in town who used to know him. Two women on separate occasions stared at him and said nothing, just wondered with their eyes if he was someone they once knew. He is just off the phone from asking Teresa to extend their holiday by a fortnight. While he had not derailed the original house sale, there had been a need for him to delay its progress. His sister likes to railroad things through and has little patience. But she had another reason to sell the house, a reason other than what she'd cited as financial pressure.

Irene's call surprises him.

'Dan,' she says.

He answers, 'Irene.'

Teasing each other with a single word – reading the tone as though it was a stepping-stone.

'I'm not going to stay on the phone for too long, Dan.'

'You think I killed Ena, don't you?'

'I do and I don't.'

'It's because I kept things from you, I understand that.'

'Let's not go over old ground. But yes, your lies were the proverbial straw....'

Silence.

'You pushed something that couldn't hack the strain and you were quite well aware what the pushing would do,' she says. 'You chose to ignore it.'

'I wanted, listen—'

'No. I won't listen. Not now, at this time. No.'

Silence.

'I think I have a pretty good idea of who killed her. He was in front of me the whole time,' he says.

'Hang on, you have a pretty good idea?'

'I think so. I don't want to say anything yet ... tell me your end.'

'Insofar ... does a car mean anything to you ... an old car ... this is all tied in to a car, I'm sure.'

'That's it?' he says. 'A car.'

'You'll find this information a big help.'

'I doubt it,' he says flatly.

'Doubt. You're good at doing that – I've told you what the cards told me.'

'Paper, bits of.'

'Spirits talk through them.'

He sighs, and says, 'I know what else they talk through.'

'Why don't you take a running jump,' she says.

'Give me a name.'

'That's not how it works.'

She kills the call.

41

Irene takes a photo of the Cliffs of Moher, buys a few postcards of the view, and some ornaments to give as gifts to her clients. She'd called Red Berry to ask if he'd gotten round to servicing her car and he said he had and it was running sweet. He was saddened to learn of her and Dan's break-up. She is numb to sympathy at this stage.

She enjoys the Atlantic air blowing into her face, its fingers running through her hair, its push against her midriff. She mingles with the other tourists, stares out at the expanse of ocean and brings her eyes to the sharp vertical rise of the cliffs. Stunning. People have stepped over the edge of these same cliffs, she imagines – these are nature's high-rise hotels, places where people wine, dine and screw before stepping, drug- and alcohol-numbed, from their balcony.

Her friend Juan Julie did it five years ago – he chose to go quickly rather than have the cancer eat away at him. He was so flamboyant – gay – a lovely man, very kind and over-sensitive.

She turns her back to the squall.

Of course Dan didn't say thanks, or acknowledge her insight as an affirmation – but then, he never had been overly supportive. Mumbo-jumbo, as far as he was concerned.

She had passed on the information. Down to him what he does with it. Such a strong impression too, from the other realm. A shout. A woman's....

Secrets breathe. Have a life of their own, even after those who carried them are dead and buried.

42

It was lovely. In the pub, at the counter, a man bought me vodka and orange and a packet of roasted peanuts. Before I'd finished the first, he bought me another vodka, and my head, after I was halfway into the vodka, began to turn funny. He was quite old and he smelt of old clothes. He asked me for my name and I told him, and where I lived, and he seemed surprised at that, as he didn't know he'd a neighbour. He lived in number 4, across the hall from my place. His name was Roger Hall and underneath us, he said, lived Percy Dunphy and Myles Carcy.

Sound lads. They were all working in town, at the local abattoir. Except for Roger – who said he worked as a forest ranger.

He wanted to buy me another, but I said I had to go. Put out by that, he grew a sour face, and changed it almost in the same instant, as if he'd caught hold of himself and told himself to cop on. The pub started to empty and I joined the queue heading out. I was glad I didn't have far to walk; I felt lovely and cosy inside. Light-headed.

I spruced up the bedsit to keep my mind off not having enough money to pay the rent next week – I'd seen a dress I liked in Molly's Boutique and couldn't resist putting a deposit down. Way too expensive, but it was lovely and blue and I used to daydream about owning a dress like that. No shoes to go with it, but I could get them later – I knew when I owned the dress I wouldn't wear it for ages and ages – I would just take it out to admire and hold it up against me. It had a little white frill around the neck and a hem of buttercups, not so big as to be garish. The woman who owned the shop said it was made for me – of course she would say that, it's her job, but it felt great to hear someone saying a nice thing about me, even if they had another reason for saying it.

The bedsit looked great after I cleaned it. I washed the curtains, the venetian blinds, the carpet, the loo, the shower and sang along to all the hits playing on the radio.

They played Bee Gees stuff and loads of other hits I could dance away to. Bloody great to have my own space, no one watching me, no bundles of clothes. I was a flower in bloom after coming out from under Mammy's shadow.

I hadn't seen her in over a week and every time I thought of her, I felt this well of pain rise up. She'd wrongly blamed me and I knew that even if she found the money or discovered the identity of the real thief, she wouldn't apologise. What she would do was she would visit me and chat to me as if nothing had ever happened. But maybe she wouldn't even do that.

I heard the knock above the music and by mistake twisted the dial the wrong way – the song shouted for milliseconds. I opened the door and standing there as bold as anything was Young Benny. He thought he had nothing to do but smile and use it to get across the threshold.

I said, 'What do you want? Fuck off!'

'I can explain,' he said, planking his hand flat against my door.

'Explain to Luigi, not me.'

'I–'

'Does your wife know that you're here?'

'Ena.'

I hissed through clamped teeth, 'If you don't get the fuck away from me, I'm going to call the guards, right?'

'I got you something.'

'I want nothing from you.'

I glared at his hand until he took it away. Slammed the door in his face and turned the radio up loud until I got a bang on the floor from the lad living underneath. I was so mad that I forgot he and another man worked nights and slept during the day. I noticed the white envelope lying on the doormat. Young Benny must have slid it in under the door; a begging letter, I told myself. Probably nowhere to live and wanted to have sex with me. Some hope.

Not a begging letter either; inside sat five hundred pounds bound with a rubber band. The notes were fresh, crisp, and smelled new. He had stolen this money from Luigi, or from someone else. Did Luigi know he was home? The money was the most stomach-settling thing I'd ever experienced. Worries gone in a flash.

I was broke and had no wages coming in, because of the advance. I'd no money to buy proper food and was eating more of Luigi's food than was good for me because it didn't cost me anything.

Part of me understood that I would be scamming Luigi if I kept the money – I was already eating his food, and keeping silent about Young Benny. But I was in a quare oul fix, as Daddy would say, and it really wasn't all my fault. My skin was covered in pimples from eating all that crap. I often felt unwell in my stomach after too, and I had a fear of getting ulcers. Or cancer even. Poisoning myself, I think.

Han was in the horrors in the chipper, in agony with her leg, she said. She wore black trousers, she told me they were the pair she'd worn to her husband's funeral, and when she'd put them on she broke out crying.

'The memory,' I said, handing her a paper cup of tea and chewing on a burger I'd made, keeping it under the counter between bites in case Luigi emerged from his office. He had gotten on to Mirror Mickey for eating a chip, so me devouring a whole cheeseburger with lashings of onions could tip him over the edge.

Luigi's health and money woes were behind him, she'd said, and he was thinking about doing up the place.

'He's taken out a new loan from the bank. I think he's going to sack me and get in another skinny young one. I hadn't realised I'd gotten so fat. Look,' she lifted her cardigan to show the swell of flesh, the trouser waist extended by a couple of two large safety pins. She went on, 'I used to have a figure like yours. It's awful what time does – you take a right good look at me, Ena – I'm not how you want to end up. A shapeless whale.'

All that yellow in her eyes probably gave her a jaundiced view of the world, poisoned all she saw.

Then she went off in her head thinking about Tom, leaving me to focus on downing my food. I didn't enjoy it: I was just filling a hole in my stomach.

When she came back from where she had been with her husband, she said, 'It's time to open up – the kids are off school today, so we shouldn't be too busy this lunch hour.'

We weren't next to being busy. A few stable lads and Dan in as the last of them left. I dried my hands on a tea towel. I was wearing a red baseball cap. I looked well, in spite of the pimples.

'Hi,' he said, smiling.

Spruced up, he was, to come into a chipper.

'Where are you off to?' I said.

'I'm going to college.'

'You go to college?'

'Leaving Cert over – I'm studying accountancy.'

'I can't remember you telling me – maybe you did.'

'In Naas.'

Twelve miles away.

'So, how are things?' he said.

'Fine, you?'

'Okay.'

Han smiled her smile at him, said to say to his mother that she was asking for her. Dan had mentioned to me at the bus stop that his mother couldn't believe Han was working in a chipper. At her age – how the mighty have fallen. She shouldn't have said that, I told him – anyone can fall on lean times. Though I hadn't met his mother, I already knew the sort she was.

Luigi came out of his hole of an office, panned his small eyes all around. Under my breath, I said to Dan that I had to look busy. Luigi was a boss who didn't care what you did, once you didn't sit or stand still on his money.

'Still okay for–' Dan said, saying what he had come in to say.

'Yes.'

He smiled. He had perfect teeth. Their dazzle made me conscious of my over-lapping eyetooth.

I watched him walk out. He had a bony arse. I liked that.

'Good-looking lad,' Han remarked.

I knew I was expected to say something. I said, 'He's okay.'

'Is he one of the Somers?' Luigi asked.

'He is,' Han said.

'Jesus – get yourself well in there, Ena … they're loaded.'

'It's not all about money,' I said, not fully in agreement with myself.

'Isn't it?' Luigi said.

He had funny eyebrows – one was straight, the other rose at a corner, as if it had broken free.

Han said, 'You're right, Ena – it's not – but I can tell you this for nothing – it helps take the sting out of living.'

Luigi leaned his elbows on the counter. The thin black forest of hairs on his forearms didn't obscure a faded blue tattoo of a harp, thick veins, and welts of flesh where he must have been burned – maybe by splashes of his own cooking oil.

'I see,' he said, 'that Young Benny is back.'

He looked at Han and then at me, searching to see if one or both of us had known.

Han said, 'Were you talking to him?'

Luigi said, 'Oh, I won't be talking to him.'

He said it as though someone else would be doing the talking for him. The guards.

'Hasn't he got some fecking nerve all the same?' Han said.

'A neck like a you-know-what,' Luigi agreed. Turning to me, knitting his fingers, he said, 'Has he been in touch with you?'

I thought the burger was going to leap up my throat and hit him in the face.

'I don't want to talk about him,' I said. 'He threw suspicion on me. And I was totally innocent.'

It was a brilliantly crafted lie.

Luigi rubbed a hand over his greasy hair, as if the lie had itched his scalp as it passed over his head.

'A … ha,' he said thoughtfully.

The right thing to do, because I realised I hadn't convinced him nearly half as well as I thought, was to ask what he

meant by his 'A … ha.' To push him for an explanation. But
he would have backed off – people around here often speak
in riddles and codes, hiding what they really feel and mean
in a layers of what they don't mean or feel. Like me.

He said to Han, 'There's a guy coming to fix the jukebox,
will you send him in to me when he comes – I'm thinking
about getting in a slot machine or two.'

He was late, and I began to think he had stood me up. The
evening was as grey as the day had been. I thought about
going home, maybe having a drink in the lounge – there
was a ballad session later on and Roger Hall said the lad
was good and would be going places. Then I spotted him.
Running, which cooled my rising anger – he was hurrying,
not sauntering. If he'd been sauntering, I'd have left him to
it.

'I'm sorry,' he said, between breaths.

'You're not fit,' I said.

'I know,' he said.

He didn't like to admit it.

He said, 'My lungs are scalded.'

'What kept you?'

'Oh … nothing.'

Nothing, in time, turned out to be his mother.

43

How do you persuade someone to rat on himself? Dan sits in the armchair in his B&B, just off the phone to Irene. The man is a shoe-in for Ena's murder, when he considers it. So obvious too. Yet it had never blipped on his radar – why was that?

He kicks off his shoes, toe to heel both times. His socks are soaked with sweat and the balls of his feet are sore. He massages each. He'd walked the town – searching out old haunts – and had been surprised at how large the town had grown in his absence. Houses in fields in which he had once played, a shopping centre here and there; Luigi's chip shop now a taxi office.

He had knocked on a few doors, but the people there weren't the ones he'd known. A couple of people who did know him had not invited him across their threshold, and each looked askance when he introduced himself with a look that said, 'What brings this fucker to my door?' Of Ena's murder, they had scant memory. There'd been a few since then, one said, half-apologetically, each as bad the last. Who could remember? The other, who'd lived in England for thirty years, said disturbingly, 'Young women, they go to these clubs and that and get sloshed and messy, end up being raped and what have you, and I say they should watch what

they drink and stuff. You can't be too careful where drink
and a crowd is concerned. They need to be responsible, yeah
mate?'

Dan said, 'And shouldn't the murderer behave
responsibly too?'

'They don't give a fuck, do they mate?'

He makes a call on a whim and arranges a day and time
to meet with Maurice Smith at the garda station – he also
elicits from him the name of a person he should visit;

Han, who'd worked with Ena, had a sister living in town.

'Where did you get my name and address?' she asks, a
scrawny woman in an overlong navy cardigan, standing just
inside the hall, her hand on the side of her front door.

'Maurice Smith. I've just gotten off the phone to him.
He said you wouldn't mind my calling down.'

'Is he still a guard?'

'He is.'

'Don't guards take a lot for granted?'

He smiles.

'Yes, I'm Joanie, Han's sister … come in.'

Over tea in her small kitchen she says, 'God forgive me
for saying this … the men who were doing you-know-what
with your wife. I'm not speaking ill of the dead, mind. But
I won't spout a lie to you either. It's not as if you don't know
it all … is it?'

But that is the thing – he doesn't know it all. He asks her
for names she might have heard, those who were 'friendly'
with Ena.

She reels off a few … one is news to his ears, one set the
chimes sounding in his head.

'Joanie … that last name, you're sure?'

'Han said it more than once. She was a talker.'

'She was a nice woman. You look a little bit like her,' he'd said as he rummaged for what else he should ask.

Nothing for now.

Back in his room, he pours himself a whiskey and stares through the window at the patchwork of roving clouds. Sips at the Jameson as he tries to get a handle on what he should do next. He reaches a decision. Barefoot, he walks to the bathroom and sits on the toilet, feeling a little unwell, and his stomach chopping at him. He rings her.

'Teresa,' he says, 'we need to talk, alone – leave Billy J. wherever it is you're staying. In an hour, at the pub here, where I'm staying, yeah?'

'What's this about?'

'Just show up.'

44

She has decided to spend two more days in Lahinch. She loves the salt air coming in off the Atlantic and the tangy smell of seaweed. Picks up several shells and puts them in her jacket pocket. Mementoes of her trip to the Emerald Isle, the wind's fingers, the old ruins of monasteries, the drab skies, the changing colours of nature, the demise of a relationship.

Their relationship destroyed by a murder. But the murder happened so long ago. She draws up short at this thought, surprised at herself for the way her thoughts had travelled, as though time diminished the terrible sin of murder. Still, let's be clear: murderers and their victims lie in the same cemetery, the truth that binds them never breaking silence.

Ena would be how old now? Fifty-one … two, three … thirty-one years dead.

God.

She will miss him. Is missing him already – her tummy is a swirl of emotion, but she remains hurt at his treatment of her and hurt also by the fact he cannot see how badly he has wounded her. In fact, when she dwells on it, he had never been one to apologise when in the wrong.

He'd an answer for everything – nothing was ever his fault. It was like playing a game of tennis with him, but only he held a racquet. He could be charming, if rarely; funny, rarer again; deep, so very much, and too frequently so. Still in love with a woman, Ena, who hadn't loved him, and perhaps therein lies the real tragedy of his life.

45

In the bedsit, I was thinking that I'd gotten into a bit of a routine over the following weeks.

A routine that I wasn't sure I wanted.

I'd meet up with Dan and we'd go the pictures or to the disco in Hotel Keadeen, in Newbridge, about thirty minutes of a journey. A privately owned bus would bring us there and back, trawling through some villages, dropping people off outside closed pubs and houses fallen dark and silent for the night. It was always packed and sometimes a row would break out and lads would be thumping the heads off each other in the aisle or lashing out from their seats – I kept Dan in at the window seat because I had an idea he wouldn't be able to handle himself in a fight; even though he said he'd boxed for a couple of seasons and won some fights.

Sometimes, the bus journeys would be fun – there'd be a singalong to songs like 'Oh, What A Night', and 'Two Tribes'. There'd even be some Christy Moore, but I didn't really like him because he sweated buckets and his lyrics were always slowly sung and a bit troubling. Dan didn't agree.

He thought the sun shone in those beads of sweat.

Another part of the routine I didn't like was Luigi and his attitude most evenings. He started to give me a hard time. His tone had changed; he was curt. A couple of times

I saw Han look from him to me. I thought she was mentally urging me to pull him up. When I failed to do that, she'd excessively shake the chips in the pan, sieving them of excess oil. She was standing up for me, but was only able to go a little way because she needed the job. She got along very well with Luigi, but now and then there was simply no getting along with him.

His heart had been badly stung, she said. Maybe it was the anniversary of his loss that made him contrary. His wife had left him for his brother, Gino. And Gino and he were identical twins. ... The town thought it strange and perplexing that a woman would have an affair with a man the spit of her husband. If she wanted a change ... Han shrugged. 'People,' she said, 'can be quare.' Even when Gino died, she didn't want Luigi back.

It was a summer's day and I'd to meet Dan at the wooded avenue that led to the Japanese Gardens, about a two-minute walk from the bedsit. I hadn't got round to telling him that I wasn't living with Mammy. He'd want to know the ins and outs of what had happened; also, I liked having a drink in the lounge before going to bed. A smoke too. It came natural to keep that little practice from him. Dan didn't like me smoking, but never made an issue out of it. I liked Roger Hall, one of the lads from the pub, and I guessed he was fond of my company. He wasn't a slimeball and I sensed he would never try anything on. He'd bought me drinks the first night in the pub, after Dan had left me home. I hadn't wanted to face into the empty bedsit and the screaming silence of its walls.

Mostly the clientele just talked, played darts, cards, or pool in an adjoining room. I was thinking too that I looked forward more to being in the pub than I did to going out with Dan – I could really relax in what Roger said was a 'convivial atmosphere'. Whereas with Dan, I occasionally got the feeling he was judging me – judging me through his and someone else's eyes.

I emerged from the bedsit, thinking it was best to be early. Last thing I wanted was for him to catch me coming out. He had the face of a combined cop and priest. Reproachful, even before you broke the law or some personal rule he thought should be one.

I closed the door, dropped the key in my denim shoulder bag. And there he stood, looking at me, a blue jacket draped over his forearm. A smile that didn't know whether to grow or wither.

'So this is it,' he said.

'What?'

'This is where you live?'

'Who told you?'

'It doesn't matter.'

'Han?'

He said nothing.

'Han,' I said.

'Why didn't you tell me?'

'Tell you what – that I'm living in a kip? Why would I be breaking my neck to tell anyone that?'

'I could help, maybe.'

'It's temporary.'

We began to walk down the path, towards the avenue.

'You're very young to be living on your own,' he said.

'I can manage. I'm almost nineteen anyway.'

'I know. In two weeks. May 20th.'

'19th,' I said.

'I was joking – I know what date it is.'

I couldn't remember his. In September, I thought. We didn't celebrate birthdays in our house.

The day could slip by without any recognition from Mammy and Daddy. Depended on how things were with them and how they were fixed money-wise.

We crossed the road. He took my hand, I dropped it. I could feel his sideways stare.

The avenue was quiet. There were lovely trees either side and horses in the paddocks. I liked grey horses and when I saw one with its head nodding over the fence, I went over, plucked a handful of grass, and held out my hand. His whiskers tickled my palm as he munched away. Dan told me to be careful, but not with the horse: the fence had been recently creosoted and was wet and smelled of fresh tar. Horses had chewed at the top of the fence, leaving large teeth imprints.

I got a large patch of tar on my jeans – they were a cheap pair and so I wasn't upset – I'd been thinking about wearing my new dress, as the day was fine, and I wanted to show myself off a little. But Dan would be thinking about where I'd gotten the money and worse, if Luigi spotted me, it would fuel his suspicion. Someone must have bad-mouthed me to him – for Luigi had the look of a man who didn't know what or who to believe anymore. I'd seen the same expression at times on Hazel's and Gilly's faces after they heard a titbit of gossip – they had difficulty accepting the truth. Everyone does, from time to time.

Dan had this small cough that hadn't anything at all to do with his chest or throat. Instead, he was nervous that I might take him up the wrong way. We were sitting at the edge of a pond, on his jacket.

I was smoking, but I was careful not to exhale in his direction.

'Do you like working in Luigi's?' he said.

'It's okay.'

'Does he pay well?'

'No. Not even fair.'

'Only....'

'What?'

'I know where there's a job going.'

'Where?'

'A chemist.'

'Which one?'

'Folan's.'

I'd never been in it.

'My mother knows the owner and she's hiring – there's no evening work involved.'

I'd seen his mother twice in the last week. Molly Somers, a large woman. She had a determined walk, like the world had better stand to one side for her. I still thought she had piles.

'Mrs Folan,' I said. 'Is that Molly?'

'I'm not sure, maybe – I only know her as Mrs Folan.'

'I see,' I said, stubbing my cigarette in the ground.

'Half-day off on a Wednesday and no Sunday work either.'

He was selling the idea, quietly.

'She'll want to see you,' he said, 'you know, to see what you think.'

To take the measure of me, I thought.

'Sure,' I said.

'Okay.'

He fell silent then, took to throwing pebbles into the pond. For a while that was the sole noise: the soft plip-plopping of stones landing in the water. We watched the ripples.

I made a few wishes. None ever reached shore: not the one for my heart to float in tranquil waters, or for the nightmares to leave me alone. They weren't even nightmares – because they sometimes came to me during the day, when my eyes were open.

46

Teresa wears grey trousers, black shoes, long amber earrings and a loose-fitting watch that had belonged to their mother. He is only putting on his shoes. She'd arrived quicker than he had expected. He had imagined some procrastination on her part, time spent thinking about what he had to say.

'What's this about, Dan?' she asks.

She carries the keys to her rental car in her left hand.

'Let's go for a drive.'

'Where?'

'I'll give you directions   come on.'

She hesitates. Clouds of uncertainty blight her features. He thinks he should ease her concerns, but doesn't have the words.

'Teresa,' he says, 'it's not far.'

Which is a lie – a short distance, yes – but in another way, it is a hell of a long route.

Her red Micra eases past the abattoir. She indicates left and enters a narrow road, following Dan's mildly delivered instructions. Furze bushes in golden bloom on one side, on the other racing stables, a derelict cottage. The road potholed with no margins and white lines.

There is a stretch of burnt-out gorse, black – a tattoo on the earth.

'Here, swing a right,' he says, pointing to a worn grass track.

'Here?' she says, nervously.

He indicates with his forefinger for her to continue past a sheep's skull.

'Anywhere, you can stop anywhere,' he says quietly, almost reverently.

She brakes. Looks across at him.

They are less than six feet off-road.

'It happened around here,' he says. 'I can't pinpoint the exact location. I doubt if there's anyone who can, even her killer.'

Her sigh is audible.

'Turn off the engine,' he says.

Sheep with red markings meander by the front of the car. In the mid-distance there is a wood of sugar pine, a man walking a bloodhound, a couple of joggers, parachutists descending from a military helicopter.

They sit in the silence until she sighs once more.

'Are you dying of something?' she asks, to the point.

'No.'

'You had a scare – Irene told me when we had a few moments alone.'

'A bad one,' he says. 'A real jolt to the body, mind and soul.'

'You got the all-clear?'

'Yeah, I did, but you're never the same afterwards,' he taps his forefinger to his temple.

'Why am I here?'

'In a minute – Irene has gone.'

'Where.'

'She left me.'

'To continue with the holiday?'

'For good ... she says.'

'Oh.'

'I kept things from her and I didn't think it would be too big of a thing to do…. But like I said, the meltdown was probably coming anyway. But I'm feeling the loss of her … I'm hoping she … anyway….'

'What did you keep from her?' she says.

He shifts on the seat, to meet with her eyes.

'My real reason for coming here.'

'Which has, let me guess, something to do with Ena and her murder?'

'He came from a large family,' he says, 'my chief suspect.'

When he notices she isn't tuning in, he says, 'A gust of wind pushed his mother out in front of a truck.'

'Yes,' she nods, and says, 'I can't remember him – but I think I went out with his older brother, Simon, was it? Once or twice.'

'He would have been ten or twelve years older than you – Mam went wild when she found out.'

'I remember. But not as wild as she did when she learned who you were dating.'

He turns his eyes to the windscreen and beyond to a string of horses en route to the gallops.

'I would have put money on this Benny being the killer,' Dan says, 'but I could never be sure….'

'Why are you telling me this, Dan?'

'A cop. Before I left for the State all those years ago. He told me about the list of suspects – Luigi O'Malley, Poncho McDonagh, Roger Hall, Benny Foster, Harry Wolfe, Don Lally, yours truly, Beth Foster, and … now I can add Billy J. I was thinking hard about him … and yeah, yeah … I should have looked at him before.'

She almost shrieks. 'Are you for fucking real – is this what you brought me out here to listen to? Bloody garbage!'

'Listen.'

'No! I won't listen – I know Billy J. and there's absolutely no way that – no … no.'

She puts her hands to her ears and then he beats her hand to the keys in the ignition.

'Give me the keys,' she demands.

'Teresa–'

'Keys!'

She opens the door and gets out of the car, storms off along the road with her hands folded across her chest. He runs after her, catches her by the upper arm and brings her to a stop.

'I'll scream, Dan,' she says.

'Go ahead. But you're involved in this too.'

'This what?' she says, her lips revealing her utter contempt.

'My wife's murder, that's what.'

She seems to resign herself and he releases his grip.

'Let's go back to the car,' he says.

He chews on his lower lip to contain his anger. She knows, he thinks, something.

Back inside the car, she reaches in the glove compartment for a packet of tissues. She is crying, an angry crying.

'Tell me,' he says.

She rubs her arm, where he had grabbed her.

'He was out on the night she was murdered – I don't know where or who he was with – he swore he wasn't with Ena.'

'He was seeing her, wasn't he?'

Teresa dabs the tissue to her eyes.

'You have no idea,' he says, 'where he was that night, do you?'

She shakes her head.

'Did you notice any change in his character at that time – was he down, angry, anything odd?'

'No.'

He says nothing for moments, giving her a little wriggle room – he is not entirely convinced she is being level with him.

'Don't lie, Teresa. I know.'

'Then why are you asking me?'

'I'm curious to find out why you stood by him.'

'Why?'

'Yes.'

'Love, what else – why did you marry Ena?'

She sniffles and blows her nose into the tissue.

He slots the keys into the ignition.

'Drive,' he says.

'What are you going to do?'

'I'm going to see Billy J.'

'No you're not – you better not hurt him. What makes you think it's him?'

'I don't, but he was someone never really ruled in for killing her, and he should have been, because he ….'

'Jesus,' she spat, her hand going to her forehead.

'I've got no intention of hurting him – unless he's the culprit, and I'm not sure he is or he isn't. But I'm going to find out.'

She scoffs. 'It could have been any one of twenty-eight men. At least.'

'It could have been a woman too,' he says.

'Whatever,' she says, taking off. 'It's great to be fucking popular, yeah?'

47

She listens to the man speak, even though she is in no mood. Last night she had dreamed about Dan and she was trying to gather its fragments. This man seemed intent on becoming her airport companion; his softly put interjections were annoying. He went on about the weather, the dreary rain, the way it greyed the small towns and villages; how it washed the smiles from people's faces; if she thinks their flight will be delayed for much longer.

'I don't know,' she says, thinking she should go for a refill of coffee. They are sitting at the same table in a crowded airport café. With luck, he might be gone when she returns. But her seat might be too. And seats are scarce.

'Are you travelling alone?' he says.

'Pardon?'

'Only, I am – and it's nice to have company – I hate flying.'

She looks at him, a man of about sixty-five with silvery hair, untamed eyebrows. He's dressed well, in blue cords and a white shirt, a light jacket thrown across his lap.

'So why do you fly, if you hate it?' she asks.

He shrugs, 'No choice – I come here to see my wife.'

'Your wife.'

He pinches the sag of his throat. 'Oh, she died ten years ago – she was visiting her parents back here in Ireland and was hit by a car while crossing the road.'

174

'Oh … I'm sorry.'

He visits her grave, she thinks, that's a hell of a round trip just to park your feet in a cemetery.

'So, I wouldn't fly, see – I was afraid – and it kept me from being with her, you know – but obviously,' he smiles, 'I got over that fear.'

She asks, 'Where are you from?'

He rubs his nose, shrugs, as though an icy drop of rainwater has fallen between his neck and shirt collar.

'I'm half Canadian, half Yank.'

'You must miss her terribly.'

He nods several times and says, 'I do, certainly', and pinches at fluff on his sweater. 'How about you?'

'I've just broken up with someone.'

'Oh, really, that's always tough.'

'Yeah, it is – and yet it isn't.'

'I follow – I was married before – it lasted six years and my,' he shakes his head, 'that was a blooper of a relationship, let me tell you.'

'My name's Irene,' she says.

'Doug,' he says.

They shake hands.

Nothing much is said for a while and then he asks what she does for a living.

'I read tarot cards.'

'That's a job?'

'It is and–'

'It isn't,' he says, smiling.

His teeth are implants, new and shiny, and his complexion the colour of an old brown boot left out in the sun for too long.

'Would you read for me? Please … I've never had it done – Erica did once – she didn't tell me much about it, though. As far as I know it wasn't a good experience. She thought the guy reading for her spoke too quickly and was only really interested in seeing her money. But I'm curious ... would you?'

'Here?' she said. 'I'm not sure. There are too many people about.... Too many different energies at play.

'I'll pay you, of course – what do you charge?'

'I–'

'Come on, it'll pass some of the time, and you'll make a few bucks.'

'Okay, but I won't charge.'

Irene closes her eyes, mentally says her prayer for protection, and says, 'Are you ready?'

'Now,' he says, his finger raised like a wand, 'I want to know the good and the bad of what the cards throw up. No holding back.'

He seems a nice man, ordinary and full of hurt like very many people. Guilt tugs at her for having been standoffish toward him. Don't be cold, she thinks.

'Okay, but I won't charge.' She hands him her deck and tells him to shuffle the pack and cut it into two hands and give the left one to her. He hands her the cards and she spreads them on the table, explaining their significance.

'Do you have a son?' she says.

'Yes, he's a doctor.'

She nods and says, 'Is there an issue with him about money?'

'Sort of,' he says, a little surprised.

'It'll end in a good way for him.'

'He'll be glad to hear that – it's a malpractice suit.'

The rest of the reading goes well, but something shows up that concerns her and she asks him to pick three cards from the other hand, to try and verify the information.

'Your health?' she says.

'Go on.'

'It's not good – have you been in the hospital lately?'

'In and out.'

'You shouldn't really be flying, should you?'

'No – this is amazing. How on earth….'

'I think you should either stay in Ireland or in the States.'

'Yeah?'

'The health card is not good, I'm afraid.'

'So what you're saying is this – if I want to be buried with my wife, I shouldn't take this plane?'

'I didn't say that, exactly.'

'It's what it means, though. I couldn't trust my son to bring my ashes to Ireland – he's so goddamn busy all the time. I'd end up in a loft or a basement in an expensive urn and be plain forgotten about.'

'I'm sorry.'

'After me getting my mouth decorated too. New teeth cost a bomb.'

She smiles.

They sit in silence. Passers-by look at them, at her deck of cards. A pack of faded cards, old, depicts angels such as Michael, Uriel, and Raphael. Not a seedy glitz pack, nor cheap, but with a gold margin and beautiful images of nature, rich with symbols that she can read and learn from as easily as someone delving into a newspaper or magazine. They were given to her by a friend whom she hasn't seen in a decade, Syl, who said she'd had a famous psychic bless them.

He stands, proffers his hand, and thanks her. Says he's going to stay on in Ireland for a little longer. The delay in taking off has stressed him somewhat and yeah, he's at an age where it's all right for him to do things off the cuff. Interesting, he says, to see how long it'll take his son to get in touch with him. To check in and see where the hell he'd gotten to.

She watches him go, a tall and gangly man that so reminds her of Louis. Her eyes drift to the cards. She collects the pack, shuffles and warns herself not to, but randomly selects three cards. There's a letter coming to her, from abroad – a purple coffin advises of a new beginning – and another is of a tall stranger in a suit, holding a bouquet of flowers, come to deliver news.

48

Luigi called me into the office on a Tuesday morning and gestured for me to sit down. He had a face like three bad winters happening at once. He brought his big hand down the length of his face and then sighed.

There were bits of Sellotape on the wall, where he used to keep a photograph of naked women showing off their bare arses. I guessed Han made him take it down. I used to think about becoming a model, but that's the problem with dreams for people like me, where I come from: dreams were what happened to other people – nightmares were what happened to us, because we were born into one and were too busy surviving it to see if we had a bigger picture.

'I've got to let you go,' he said, eyes falling to the wire bin full of crumpled notepaper and an unravelled typewriter ribbon.

He was having a hard time hanging on to his skin, I could tell. I thought of Han, how she'd been kind of distant when I arrived in for work. Her 'Hello' subdued and her expression locked in neutral. She knew about this and hadn't tipped me off.

'Young Benny told me,' he said,

'What has he got to do with me?'

'He said it was your idea to rob the money – that he gave you some of the takings.'

He pushed back his chair and angled it to the narrow window that looked out at nothing much – a bare concrete wall a foot or two away. There were spots of Tipp-ex on the desk. His old typewriter squatted on top of a grey cabinet whose doors couldn't shut.

'Do you believe him?' I said, a shade indignantly.

He put his small finger in his ear, wriggled it, and said, 'He gave me back the money and said you had the rest of it – is that true, yeah?'

'No,' I said, 'he most certainly did not.'

'No?' he said, his tone implying that he doubted very much what I'd said. 'Really? His wife said she herself counted out the money and put it in the envelope and slid it under your door.'

'She's lying.'

'Why would she – tell me?'

'Because they don't have the rest of the money and she doesn't want the prick to go to gaol.'

He puckered his lips.

'Maybe,' he said.

'And when did she say they gave me the money?'

'Very recently, at your bedsit.'

I was sure Beth hadn't been with Young Benny when he called round, though she could have been waiting for him outside or in the pub.

'Well, I've got most of my money back – and I won't be taking the matter further with the guards. His wife seems a nice woman and I like to give people a break – more fool I, sometimes. Clever woman she is that she got my money back in return for me not pressing charges.'

His stare was hard.

'Can I say something?' I said.

He held out his hand, palm out. The floor was mine.

'Why would they give me money?'

'Your share, maybe?'

'Five hundred quid. My share?'

It took me seconds of swallowing his glare to realise I'd put a Charlie Noose around my neck.

'I never said how much was in the envelope,' he said.

I felt as though the ground at my feet had turned to lava and was running up my legs, my body, and filling my neck and cheeks with a crimson glow.

'I didn't know what to do with it – I swear I wasn't involved with him cleaning you out. I swear.'

'Your mother … what happened there?'

I didn't say, because he knew, and he could only have found out from Mammy or Han, or whoever Mammy had told.

He said, 'You just told me that you had a big row with her – you never said what about.'

'I didn't steal money from anyone.'

'According to Benny, you guys used to short-change customers, that yous had a ball when I was in dock with my kidneys.'

'He did that, overcharge.'

'You didn't tell me.'

I couldn't think of an excuse for not doing that and I said, 'Sorry, I should have upped and said. But how was I to know he was going to rob you like that, of so much? I mean….'

'Go on?'

'Nothing.'

'You two were more than good friends, according to Beth – his wife. According to Young Benny.'

A light bulb flicked on in my head. The fucker had spilled his guts to Beth about our fling.

'Get your jacket, and bring me my money. Don't be expecting a week's wages.'

'Luigi….'

'On your bike.'

When I put my hand on the chrome door handle, he said, 'He said he had sex with you behind the counter. Is that part of his story true?'

I inhaled a deep breath, so deep I could smell the blue paint on the door, though it was six months old. Facing him, I said, 'You could have done the same Luigi, if you'd asked.'

This shocked and excited him. His eyes took on a wildness.

'Do you want to work off what you owe me?' he said.

'Fuck off, Luigi.'

I went out and slammed the door behind me. Han looked at me, but I didn't acknowledge her. I promised I would never acknowledge her again.

Problem was, I no longer had Luigi's money. It was hanging from the wardrobe in my bedsit, above a pair of high-heels and alongside a new pair of jeans. So, I sat on my bed and then I lay on it, and then got up and drank half a bottle of vodka and slept the day through, until evening.

Roger Hall knew by me that I was in bad form. It was Tuesday evening and the pub was quiet. The telly was on in the corner, *Mork and Mindy*, but no one was paying it any heed. He bought me a drink and I said, 'Thanks,' and he asked who had died belonging to me.

'No one,' I said.

He stubbed his cigarette out in the green Heineken ashtray. He was growing a moustache and I wasn't sure if it suited him. I think that was the first evening I noticed how good looking he was, in an old-man-ish sort of way. The word mature came to mind.

'The boyfriend dump you?'

'No – I'm not seeing him until Friday. He's got to study for exams.'

He nodded, put a hand to his half-full pint glass.

'Something wrong there,' he said, before taking a swallow.

I watched the liquid move down his throat.

'What do you mean?'

'That he would rather study than spend time with a beautiful-looking girl like yourself.'

I felt flattered but I used to like his company because he wanted nothing else; now, I sensed there was a turn in him.

He bought me another drink and a packet of dry roasted peanuts. Two old guys in the space of a few hours were after lighting on me. Our fingertips met at the mouth of the opened pack.

The next morning, after he'd gone from my bed, I felt so alive. He'd opened the curtains before leaving, and kissed me on the forehead. There were some notes spread on the bedside locker, enough to make up the rent for Kevin, my landlord, who'd warned me last week about being late.

'Friday, not Monday, Ena. That's our arrangement.'

Grumpy old so-and-so.

I stretched my legs. I was sore around the ribs from the weight of Roger and reeked of Old Spice aftershave and Brylcreem. He'd sweated a lot – as if he was being held over a roasting fire. Maybe he was, in a way. I thought it might hurt like it had with Young Benny, but no. It was just so lovely. When I came, I bit him on the neck.

Later, he told me I was never ever to do that again.

49

They are staying in a cottage outside town, near an old folk's home, she says. Dan reckons that it must be like living in a shed for the pair, they who were so accustomed to a more opulent residence. His sister sighs frequently as they edge past traffic lights outside the cemetery where Ena is buried. He blesses himself. Teresa glances at him and says, 'Since when?'

'Since when, what?'

'You went back to being a believer?'

'I'm paying my respects, that's all.'

'She treated you like shit.'

'So did a lot of other people.'

'Not next to nor the manner in which she did.'

'You treated me shabbily, too – my own sister, flesh and blood.'

'Everyone saw that she was bad for you – that she was going to bring you down. She did, too.'

'Well, she wasn't a piece of cake to live with, that's for sure.'

'And she drove a wedge between you and Mam.'

'That was already there.'

'Ena made matters worse, then.'

'I saw the potential in her.'

'What potential – she was a slut.'

'Don't say that. Don't.'

'Why not? It's the truth – you almost killed her for being one.'

'I loved her.'

'No, you love her.'

'If you know that, why insult her?'

'Because....'

'You want to hurt me.'

She indicates, eases into a small tarred yard, and parks. When he gets out of the car, he smells roses, their fragrance rich and invigorating, but he can't see any bushes.

'Are there roses around the back?' he asks, looking about at the tiny yard with its narrow verges devoid of flowers and shrubs.

'Nothing only knee-high grass.'

Something their mother used to say about a saint, Teresa, she announced her presence through the scent of roses. She used to wear a silver medal with a dot of fabric from the saint's habit encased in Perspex, around her neck.

'Neighbours?'

'About a half mile away.'

She turns the key in the front door and walks ahead of him, down a hallway into a kitchen that seems full of shadows. Billy J. is sitting at a table covered with a cheap plain oilcloth, a broadsheet newspaper spread before him.

'This is a surprise,' he says, folding the paper.

'He thinks you killed Ena,' Teresa says.

The statement lingers in a silence shrouded with dim light and a pervading iciness.

Finally, Billy J. says in a low tone, 'What makes you think that?'

'Not what. Who. Teresa,' Dan says, 'and an old woman, Joanie Kelly, with a memory given to her by her sister, Han. Name ring a bell?'

50

Halfway across the Atlantic, according to the flight route on the monitor, Irene is disturbed from her thoughts by the young man beside her, who needs to use the loo. She turns off the screen, looks to the right at the young man's girlfriend, who smiles at her and then returns to watching her movie.

Irene's feet suddenly feel the cold and she eases her toes into her slip-ons. There is a stabbing pain in her chest when she remembers that Dan had sat next to her on the outward flight.

She misses his presence, his quiet self-assurance, his wry smile, the mischievous sparkle that too rarely comes to his eyes. What hurts her, perhaps always will, is his silent and persistent hankering after his first wife. His hanging on to the coat tails of what had been a miserable existence for him. She had thought to say this to him during an argument, but dared not: that he revelled and thrived in being treated like shit.

He cannot see beyond the past. Conversely, she admires him for the way he is intent on clearing his name – in spite of the fact that many of his contemporaries from that era are dead. She stands up to let the young man return to his seat.

She is quick to resume her line of thinking.

Dan had told her that his cancer scare had triggered a perfect storm within him.

'I also feel,' he'd said, 'as though it has thrown crumbs of bread to a flock of pigeons.'

Seeing that she didn't pick up on the analogy, he went on. 'My thoughts are the pigeons and the bread signifies crumbs of truth.'

He was none too impressed at her saying it was a very Jesus-y thing for him to come out with.

'I think your scare should have made you aware of your own mortality – you need to be doing new stuff.... Visiting new places, giving us both good memories, yeah?' she'd said.

'Look, Irene – she didn't deserve to die like that, no one does.'

'I agree with you. But it was a long time ago.'

But he wouldn't let it go. He was worse than a dog after getting the bone of his dreams. Some couples have a mother-in-law as the third party in their marriage, she had a dead wife.

'He's gotten away for it for far too long,' he'd said.

'He? You know the killer?'

'Not yet. Can you look into the cards and read the past?'

There was a sarcastic look to his features but she wouldn't rise to it.

'Well, it would be great if I could, because the past, I'm learning, holds more secrets than the present and future put together.'

51

I was in bad form the whole night and Dan thought it was because of him. I wasn't mad at him, but I'd been thinking about breaking things off, telling him I needed a break, making it sound like we could start seeing each other again, in a few weeks. But I couldn't bring myself to do it, not after he'd told me I'd gone down a bomb with Kitty Folan and that I had landed the job, and to say nothing to anyone about it because she wanted to tell me first. Roger Hall had a word for me with Kevin too, and I was sorted for a part-time job in the pub. It wouldn't pay much to begin with, but after I was trained in, Kevin said he'd look at a raise then.

'You come highly recommended,' he'd said.

This meant he hadn't been talking to Mam, her cronies, Han, Luigi or Young Benny's wife.

I had an idea that Beth, or the lot of them combined, caused my reputation the most harm.

I should have been delighted. Two jobs. Sorted. But, I dunno, I felt gloomy inside – and I thought it had something to do with Roger, that he'd shafted me with a stick of black depression.... I felt really, really down. Every time I'd grow a smile, it would slide off my face.

We were dancing to Skid Row in Hotel Keadeen and Dan was away eating the supper that came with the admission.

Peas, sausages and mash. I wasn't hungry and I doubt if he was, but he wouldn't pass anything by that was free or he had paid for. I liked the band – the guy with the long hair, the lead singer, was cute. I noticed this guy looking at me from the bar. While I knew him from somewhere, I couldn't recall where from or what his name was. He kept on staring, making me feel uncomfortable; every notch on my spine warned me to get out from under that stare.

What was keeping Dan? Was he still in the dining area, pigging out?

Then a nice-looking guy asked me to dance and I said yes, and we took to the floor. I was wearing my new skirt and though Dan liked it, I could tell he wasn't too happy that it ended right under my bum. A blue miniskirt. I thought it looked great. The guy spoke to me; I couldn't hear above the music, and I was on the lookout for Dan and keeping an eye on our drinks. The set of three ended and the band took a break and the DJ talked about a slow set. I thanked the fella and retuned to my table.

No sign of Dan. I was getting thick and thought I should have stayed on the floor. The guy with the stare was still staring. And then his name came to me, Don Lally … Mirror Mickey. Mickey. The guy who'd briefly worked for Luigi; who believed he'd owned the feeling rights to my arse. He still needed a mirror to look below the waist.

He was plastered and staring at the world through a mist of Guinness.

I ignored Dan when he came back. Just continued looking directly ahead, wondering if that was Gilly over in the corner with Wally Snyder. It wasn't.

'Are you okay?' Dan said, leaning forward in his chair, hand on the table, drumming to the beat of the song.

'Grand.'

I sipped at my black Russian, took out the lemon and sucked at it.

'The supper was nice.'

It's all about your belly tonight, I thought.

Oh Christ – his fat hand was out, his belly as huge as it had been when he worked in Luigi's.

'Dance, Ena,' he said.

He had a mop of curly black hair. His eyes were hazy and his lips wet. His forehead filmed with sweat.

'I'm with someone,' I said.

He wagged a finger at me. 'I heard,' he slobbered, 'all about you.'

He tapped the side of his nose with his forefinger. His head seemed to swivel in Dan's direction.

Between hiccups, he said, 'I know you …' he clicked his fingers, 'don't tell me,' hiccup, 'Somers – I knew your father, I did' – hiccup – 'a nice man, a gentle fucking man, is what he was,' hiccup. 'She with you, yeah? Lucky man, lucky man … I tell you. I….'

'Dan?' I said, nodding at the dance floor.

We skirted past Mirror Mickey and danced a slow set in the thick crowd.

'He's freaking me out,' I said.

'I think that skirt is making all the fellows wild.'

I read a slight hint of reproach in his tone – it matched the look he had given me when we met at the bus stop.

'Really?' I said into his ear. 'Or is it what's underneath?'

It was funny to see him go scarlet. I think he came close to swallowing his tongue. I gave him the green light, because being in the disco with Mirror Mickey was making me uncomfortable – his eyes were doing the walking for his fingers. And I didn't want him coming up to Dan and saying stuff about Young Benny and Beth and that – filling Dan's head full of questions.

'Let's go outside,' I said.

'Sure,' he said, 'but there's still an hour left....'

'It's a warm night.'

It got warmer. He was stronger than I imagined and I could feel him hard as through his jeans ... he was rough with me in that dark corner. No sign of the nice mammy's boy. After brushing his hand away, I gave in to its return visit and dropped my knickers while he lowered his jeans. I guided him into me. He came after around three seconds, just as I was beginning to get going. He was breathing hard.

I was hoping Roger Hall might be waiting up for me and I felt bad thinking that – what sort of girl was I? Dancing with the devil.

After moving from the dark corner, I lit up a smoke and asked him if he was okay. He remained silent. He was thinking about other things ... stuff he would later throw at me.

52

'You're serious,' Billy J. says. 'Unbelievable.'

Dan can't sit still and moves to the edge of his seat. He studies him, waiting for words to happen. He is restraining himself from physically attacking Billy J. He feels the strain constrict his throat, and cause a niggling pain in his midriff.

'Teresa gave you an alibi for the night of Ena's murder,' Dan says.

'Yes,' Billy J. admits, eyeing Dan. 'I won't deny it. Who told you?'

'You were hauled in for questioning, as I was. It came to me – I was wandering the town, beating on a few doors, and names kept dropping into my mind. Yours landed too. Joanie Kelly – she filled in the blank spaces.'

Teresa says, 'Dan....'

Dan sees the tension on her face; her eyes look furtive, haunted and fearful.

'I'll make coffee,' she says, filling the kettle.

'You asked her to give you an alibi too,' Billy J. says quietly, accusingly.

'The first night,' Dan says, 'when I ... but she didn't give it – I didn't ask for her one when Ena was killed. She offered me one, though. I thought that quite a turnaround.'

Water gushes into the blue kettle.

'He is my husband,' she says.

She plugs in the kettle.

'And you were protecting him,' he says.

Silence.

'So, I'm waiting,' Dan says. 'I'm your brother. What is it you said to me – you would never lie for anyone – face the music, that's what you said.'

'I didn't think you needed one – everyone knew what sort of woman she was – no court would have convicted you for thumping her. She – Mam – was going crazy at the thoughts of you and her, the talk of the town it was. It hurt her badly – she couldn't believe you'd stoop so low in your choice of partner.'

'But that was the thing – she was my choice.'

'Your mistake.'

'As it turned out – but if I'd taken her away from here....'

'Listen to yourself,' Teresa says, in a biting tone.

'Baloney,' Billy J. says, 'she was carved out of bad stuff.'

'Shut it! You're on thin ice,' Dan says.

Billy J. shakes his head. He hasn't shaved, and the window light shows up a thin growth of silvery blond hair.

'So, I'm waiting,' Dan says.

Billy J. studies his hands. 'A few months before Ena was killed I was brought in for questioning by the guards – for sexual assault on a woman who is living in Australia. I was drunk and as guilty as hell afterwards – I gave her money to stop her going to the cops.'

'She took it,' Teresa says, taking milk from the fridge, 'and then went ahead and made the allegation. I had to step in, didn't I? The guards would have had him pinned as a chief suspect for Ena's murder and hauled him over the coals. I had to think of Mam and what it would do to us and our reputation.'

'But,' Dan says, leaving the word hang until it draws their attention to him, 'you went out and stalked this woman, and you made it sound as though you chanced upon her … you didn't, it was a premeditated attack.'

'I was drunk and mad at her, yeah – I just wanted to put the frighteners on her, to leave us alone.'

'She was continually blackmailing him – us,' Teresa says.

'Why?' Dan says.

Nothing is said while Teresa spoons the coffee into mugs.

'Well?' Dan prompts.

'I was having an affair with her,' Billy J. says, throwing his hands in the air. 'Are you happy now?'

Teresa says stiffly, 'There's more – tell him.'

'She was pregnant, she said … it was a lie.'

Parallels here, Dan thinks, with what happened between himself and Ena.

'So,' he says, 'you wanted to frighten her off – this is what you're passing off as the truth?'

'It is the truth,' Teresa says, her tone tuning to a sharp singing blade, 'but she was one of a few – isn't that right, Billy J.? How many?'

He doesn't answer.

'Where do you think our money went,' Teresa asks Dan, 'only on keeping him out of trouble – paying off his whores and bastards.'

Billy J. digs at the tiled floor with his eyes.

'I didn't want Mam to find out – it would have killed her – her heart wasn't good, you know that,' Teresa says.

'We upped and left, not long after Ena's murder,' Billy J. says.

'Which also got me to thinking – that was a suspicious move.'

'You left too,' Teresa reminds him, 'we left after you killed our mother.'

Billy J. says, 'Teresa....'

'What? He bloody did – there was the shame he brought to us by associating us with that slapper and then she went and highlighted it to the world by getting herself killed – do you remember the fucking press, the TV cameras? The way people in town were talking? It destroyed Mam.'

'I used to think that,' Dan says, 'but not any longer.'

'No?' Teresa says. 'Well, good for you.'

'I was with Ena when she died – I was in hospital with her.'

The only noise is that of Teresa pouring water into the mugs. It is as though the kitchen is holding its breath.

'She came to for moments. I don't think she recognised me,' he continues. 'I sometimes like to imagine that she did, that she told me who was responsible – didn't happen, of course. I told her that it wasn't me ... I said it over and over, but her eyes were glazed and she ... I think she was blind.'

'That was tough on you,' Billy J. says.

'The coffee is ready,' Teresa says.

'She wasn't raped – she couldn't possibly have seen who had hit her with the brick.'

Teresa says, 'And who told you that – your new wife, the self-styled fortune teller?'

'No – forensics – after they'd established that I hadn't killed her.'

'You thought it was me,' Billy J. says in disbelief, 'seriously?'

'They blamed Roger Hall and that tinker, what's his name, Poncho McDonagh, and Don Lally and who else ...' Teresa says, picking up her coffee.

'A so-called Young Benny and Beth, his wife – do you remember her?' Dan says.

'Hmm, low-lifes, the pair of them.'

'I'm sure there were more suspects too,' Billy J. says, 'I mean....'

'Yes – there were a few who, for whatever reason, never came into the reckoning.'

'I said that to you earlier on,' Teresa says.

'Yes, you did, in your own inimitable way.'

Billy J. gets to his feet, digs his hands into his pockets. He walks to the counter, puts a spoon of sugar into his mug, stirs. Teresa distances himself from him. Sits in an armchair by a wood stove that has fractured glass, crosses her legs and wraps her hands around the mug.

'Teresa?' Dan says.

'Yes.'

'You provided an alibi not just to save Billy J. – you knew if Mam heard about the allegation, she might have cut you out of her will altogether.'

Silence.

'Why did you offer to give me an alibi for the night of Ena's murder?' he says.

'Mam asked me. I suppose she was sure you'd killed your wicked darling.'

'You're every bit as bloody wicked.'

'Is there more?' Billy J. says quietly.

'I spoke with Joanie, Han Kelly's sister.'

Billy J. says, 'I can't place her.'

Dan continues, saying this as bait to lure information, 'And to the guard, Maurice Smith....'

Silence.

'Why don't you tell me?' Dan says sternly.

53

Red Berry calls over about five minutes after she'd turned on the light in the kitchen. Stands there on the veranda, his lean head framed by a pillar post, the night sky and its stars. He dangles the spare set of house keys and says, the other hand hidden from view, 'I done the car and it's running like an ace, like I said.'

'Thanks, Red,' Irene says.

She is tired and wants to shower and get to bed, but....

'You want a nightcap?' she says, hoping he might decline the offer.

'I wouldn't say no.'

'Come in.'

He brings his hand from behind his back, where a bunch of white roses is held, and says, 'I know you like them and I think they'd make for a nice smell to meet you in the kitchen come morning.'

'Red, they're gorgeous,' she says, holding them, drawing in their freshly watered scent.

She goes ahead of him into the large sitting room, skirting her luggage, and moves her jacket from the armchair Red likes to sit on when he visits. He used to get lonely when his wife died and he shared that loneliness a lot at the beginning. Now he endures it by himself, because, he often says, time has taught him how. Tall, with ginger strands of hair spread across his crown, he is sparsely built, dresses mostly in loose-fitting jeans and a blue denim shirt with those pearl buttons Irene doesn't like.

He sits in the armchair and watches her put the flowers in a glass vase she'd half-filled with water. Withdrawing her hand, she pricks her finger in a thorn and a speck of her blood lights on a white petal – blood upon the rose – she isn't sure if that is a good sign. Probably the same as a black cat crossing your path: opinion differs as to what sort of luck it brings.

Red hands her a tissue. 'Is it lodged in the skin? Does it need a tweezering?'

'No,' she replies, dabbing the tissue to her finger.

She goes to her handgrip, surfaces a bottle of duty-free Powers Whiskey and says, 'I got you this, Red, but don't be skulling the lot in one go.'

'Can't do that anymore,' he says, 'wish the hell I could – but we'll break this seal, yeah, and make a toast. I'll get the tumblers.'

They touch glasses and say nothing. Ice cubes clink as they sip.

'So, you said you're leaving,' Red says.

'I am.'

'No hope of saving the…?'

'No.'

'That's sad. I liked both you guys very much.'

'It's for the best. He hid too much from me. I think he'll always be hiding stuff from me.'

He sighs, pats the armrest gently. 'Maybe so. Anyhow, you're a big girl, and you know better than anyone what's kicking in …' he taps his chest lightly. 'I'll miss you, can't say I won't. A good neighbour is a priceless thing'

'Thank you, Red. You were a good neighbour too.'

He finishes his drink and sets the glass on the coffee table. 'I'll be on way before I get maudlin – best we say goodbyes now – I hate a long-drawn affair.'

'Will you hang on to the spare keys until Dan gets back?'

'Sure.'

He stands, and they hug, and she sees him out, guessing he'll slaughter that bottle.

Plan is, she thinks, to sleep well, get up and shower and set to packing. She needs a clear head, as she doesn't want to remember something halfway down the highway and have to come back for it. Nor does she want to ask Dan for anything. Best if the break is clean. She has an apartment in mind – going to be busy for a while, touching base with her clients, getting the feel of a new home. She'd considered packing before retiring to bed, thinking to get a head start, but understood she'd suffer for it later. Suffering...

54

I liked working in the pharmacy. The pay was better than in the takeaway and I didn't go home stinking of greasy batter and fish. Instead, I smelled of perfume and deodorant. The customers were different to those who came into the chipper, or I should say their attitude was different, because some of the customers were also regulars of Luigi's. They were quieter, more subdued, or so it seemed – certainly weren't as friendly toward me as they had been when I was serving them from across Luigi's counter. Han and Luigi had probably bad-mouthed me to them, and they might have thought I had some nerve for trying to better myself – Kildarragh people can be funny, and not hah-hah funny, either.

Kitty Folan was easy to work for, after a few weeks that is, when she saw her takings weren't down any. I wasn't allowed to dispense prescriptions – that was a total no-no. I was to be the smiling face behind the counter, taking the forms and passing them on to her or her sister, Mrs Frieda Watson.

I got my hands on a box of condoms when a salesman gave Frieda free samples – she was totally anti-contraception, called the condoms disgusting and told me to throw them in the bin out the back.

When she got to hear about it – I don't know who told her – maybe Frieda herself – Kitty had war with her, telling her older sister they'd to move with the times and she was to leave her conscience and judgemental attitude at home. I learned from the sisters' comments that Dan's mother was best friends with Frieda and not Kitty.

I needed the rubbers and to go on the pill, which Dan thought I was taking. I had to tell him, because he'd asked – and I don't know – maybe lying is a disease, for everytime anyone asks me a question I seem to come out with a lie. I'm a natural-born liar, I think. VD, too … another reason for the johnnies. That fanny scare, Jesus, if it happened, would be a complete and utter disaster. Dan would be as clean as, but Roger was a different story. I'd thought to warn Roger off by telling him I had an STD, but in the end I realised it wouldn't bother him.

I couldn't allow matters to keep on going as they were – not with Roger and Dan coming into me. I'd daydream occasionally that it wasn't possible for me to conceive, but knew I was being plain silly. It wasn't a question of if, just when. The first few weeks were full of scares in the chemists. My period was delayed and I swore to myself that nothing would get inside me unless it was wearing protection. But even they weren't completely safe. Gilly said she used rubbers, and look at her, three months gone and her parents were forcing her to get married – she loved Sny, so she was lucky in that regard – and he loved her.

'Still, what if they didn't love each other?' I'd said. 'What then?'

Gilly'd shrugged.

'Don't rely on the johnnies,' she'd warned.

The other scare happened when I was stacking a shelf with bottles of sun cream, and through the window, I saw Luigi crossing the road. He'd called down to the bedsit a couple of times, but went away after I didn't respond to his raps on the door and calls of my name. I excused myself and went to the loo – I was steaming too – how dare he chase me to my new workplace? As it turned out, he was only leaving in a prescription for his blood pressure. I had to keep a watch out for him, all the same … I liked the job and didn't want to lose it.

I preferred working in the pub. It had a more relaxed atmosphere than the chemist, and after six months I was shit-hot, as Roger Hall said, at pulling a pint and dealing with customers. I could sing too, a little, and shoot pool. Kevin increased my wages and matched it against an increase in the rent. This soured Roger enough for him to pull him up on it.

Kevin said he could like or lump it, and what's more, it was none of his business – a month later, Kevin's four tyres were slashed outside a theatre in Dublin. Gut instinct told me that Roger had either done it, or seen to it that it was…. Kevin had an inkling too: he acquired a suspicious and peculiar way of looking at Roger, when Roger wasn't aware, a wondering look.

There was a sprinkling of odd customers in the pub: people down on their luck, some with hard faces, others cold, others with eyes that were moist, as though primed to cry, but never would because life had bled those ducts dry. Some liked to talk to me, just to pass time, were friendly, and there were those who sat silently at a table by their pint, looking at it as though it was someone who had never let them down. Scary men, too – these wore poker faces and I could never tell what it was about them, only knew it was best to keep them like books you see in huge libraries in big houses, on the shelf nearest the ceiling, where they ought to be – left unread. Men who were friendly, cracking jokes, but in the cracking I sensed a couple were searching for a way forward with me, and that this could be judged by my smile, a laugh, a look: they wanted to pick up a crumb of encouragement. Old fellas with bellies that hung like cliff ledges over their genitals, disgusting – and then there were others who had a peculiar appeal and these men, not many – two or three … much older than me, assured, experienced, had tales to tell, and they seemed to be fearless. I think the attraction concerned their lack of fear, and their aura of being at home in the world: no matter what life threw at them, they would handle it. Occasionally I would catch their eyes and see trouble flash in their irises, and I would always feel a tingle of excitement race up and down my spine. Then there were bad thoughts I had to frantically push way away from me; it was like I was suddenly surrounded by a mass of bluebottles and they were buzzing and plotting a way past my waving hands and zipped lips.

I cleaned the toilets and the smell of piss used to sicken me so much I took to wearing a scarf around my nose and mouth. Men were dirty bastards. You could have emptied lovely spray from a dozen canisters in the jacks and the smell of piss would find a way through in about five seconds flat.

We closed for a half day on Wednesdays and I was crossing the road to the boutique as I'd to collect a new jacket when I bumped into Mammy. I looked smart in myself, was after getting my hair cut and styled, so I didn't mind her seeing me. I wanted her to see that I was thriving without her. She weighed me up and down and I felt sorry for her in her old clothes – wrinkles were beginning to cut deep into her face too. I showed her my new tattoo and she said I was fucking mad as ever and who had heard of black roses.

'Why didn't you get red? Of course, that'd be you being normal.'

'Always the kind word.'

'Someone is doing well for herself,' she said, her lips pursing.

'I'm doing okay.'

'Not pregnant at least – which is something, I suppose.'

'I left the chipper.'

'I heard.'

'I'm going out with Dan Somers.'

I don't know why I said that – maybe to impress her – the Somers were highly thought of in town, while we were lowly thought of. Some might say to be regarded as low was too high for us.

'And what does his mother think of that?

'I haven't met her.'

'Have you been introduced to her?'

I remained silent.

She looked at me and said, 'That should tell you something.'

I let that go, because she was spot on. She had fresh vegetables in her shopping bag, market-bought – I saw the earth on the carrots, smelt the strawberries.

'Luigi told me you owe him some money,' Mammy said. 'He stopped me outside the church last Sunday to tell me.'

'I'll pay him back.'

That fucking weasel – hammering on my door last week, putting a note under it to say he knew I was inside, that he wanted his money back. To pay him back a little every week, to call in to see him to make that arrangement. I wondered, if I told Roger about him, would he get Luigi off my back?

'Do – I don't want his kind bothering me.'

'His kind?'

'He's a dirty old man – I'm sure you learned that much about him.'

'He never behaved in a dirty way with me.'

At least not with his hands, I thought.

She had a cautious look in her eye, as though she'd things to say but wasn't too sure if she should. I reminded myself that though she was my mother, she had not come looking for me after our bust-up. I liked to think she had kept a watch from afar, but that, I thought, was about as fanciful as the notion that I couldn't be made pregnant.

Spits of rain began to fall and I didn't want to get my hair wet, so I said I better head, that it was going to lash out of the heavens.

She said, 'You're working in a pub too.'

'Word gets around. You can't piss crooked in this town but everyone gets to know.'

'You must be rolling in it.'

'I'm not.'

'You're fond of the boutique.'

'God, you must have spies everywhere.'

'Ah, sure people always found it natural to talk to me – they think you're still at home, I suppose. They don't ask though, if you are or not.'

'Why didn't you tell them I'd left?' I said, knowing she had.

She said nothing.

'And, Mammy, do you know something else?'

'What?'

'I didn't steal a cent – you blamed me in the wrong. And you won't admit to it. Because if you thought I had, you'd be looking for me to pay you back first, ahead of Luigi.'

Her shoulders went up and down, her chin sort of dug in, like it used to before Daddy would belt her.

'Harry owned up a while back,' she says. 'I threw him out – I think he told me because that's what he wanted me to do. He can't make a decision for himself.'

'And you wouldn't tell me,' I said.

'I–'

'Did you mention this to the gossips you blackened me to?'

Silence.

'No,' I said, 'you bloody didn't.'

Maybe I would have said more, but the rain served as a full stop.

'Mammy,' I said, shaking my head before walking away.

'Ena,' she called.

'What?' I said, turning about.

'Bring him down to see me, your man – Somers. Sunday, come for tea. Do.'

'What time?'

'Sixish.'

'I'll think about it.'

Mammy said something but I didn't hear, as I was too busy getting in out of the rain.

An hour later, I was in my bedsit, listening to the radio, and thinking about Dan – we were to meet with his sister and her boyfriend in the pub that evening. Dan had got to hear I was working a second job and he wanted to know why I hadn't told him. I said I wanted to surprise him, but only when I was fully trained, and when certain I was going to stick at it. I'd rang Roger at his workplace and could hear all of these people guffawing at him in the background, saying the young one he was knocking off was on the line. I could hear him telling them to fuck off, saying it with humour, his tone full of pride.

'What's up?' he'd said.

'Roger, I ... my boyfriend and his sister and....'

'Your what?'

Jesus, I thought – what did he think? That I was his and his alone?

'He's....'

'I'm kidding,' he said, 'I saw you with him before – I'll keep my distance from you, don't worry.'

But I was worried. Obviously he'd been talking to his pals. He'd sworn he would keep us a secret, but maybe he had opened his mouth – his workmates who lived underneath us would have heard us in action above the volume of my TV; I thought of the squeaking bed, the moans. I was worried about being found out; but I had no guilt. That worried me too. Its absence was telling me the sort of person I had become.

I think I'd lost the reins of myself the very instant I had stepped into Luigi's chipper to ask him for a job.

55

He lets what he has just said hang in the silence.

Billy J. sighs, then says with some exasperation, 'Yes … okay … you want the fucking truth so much, then I'll give it to you – I was with Ena a couple of times.'

Teresa snorts and looks into the unlit stove.

Dan says, 'My wife.'

'I know that – but she wasn't, was she, not really – and hadn't been for a while….'

Dan watches his sister, notices how pale she has become, the stare – she is merely half-listening, distancing herself from hearing words that had long before torn at the fabric of her soul. Stirring within him, too, are memories of why he had followed Ena and beaten her – he can almost feel the slash of her fingernails across the side of his neck, hear her scream, the temper high in her as she tried to yank off his black balaclava – he who had wanted to scare her back into his arms, had himself ended up being terrified by her tenacious defence. She believed she was fighting for her life – only he knew she wasn't. Such a stupid thing for him to do – half out of his mind with drink, a spot of hash … stupid … stupid. A distorted and harried thought pattern. He'd often thought, perversely, that he had given her a warning, advance notice.

'She wasn't, no,' he agrees, reflectively, sadly. His anger dissipating by degrees.

'How can you be here, dealing and worrying us with this,' Teresa asks, 'after the way she treated you – where does that trait of forgiveness come from? Not from Mam, that's for sure, or from Dad … he would've been put out with you big time.'

'I'm here because this time last year I thought I'd be dead within weeks – I'm here because I've lived under the shadow of not having the answers for far too long, here because she didn't deserve to die like that, and because if the killer is alive I want him brought to justice.'

Nothing is said. Outside, there is a flurry of birdsong.

'I didn't kill her,' Billy J. says, standing, going to the back door. 'I need to have a smoke.'

To Teresa, he says, 'Tell him – tell him, for God's sake – and be done with it.'

'Teresa,' Dan says.

Billy J. closes the door behind him. He stands on the step, leaves it.

'Teresa,' Dan says.

56

I loved drinking and being with men who made me laugh. Some of them that is: the ones I could relax with, those who didn't make it obvious they were looking for something in return.

What most of the villagers thought didn't bother me. I had other things on my mind. That afternoon I'd been coming out of the boutique when I spotted Luigi. I went in the opposite direction to avoid meeting him – he would have had my IOU pinned to his tongue and licked me with it. He didn't know how to let money stay lost. God knows I did want to pay him back, but there was always something to draw my money elsewhere. Like buying a nice top or skirt to make myself feel good, even when I knew that the good feeling wears off after its first wearing.

Just round the corner, haunting his lips with a fag, was that Owen Noctor. My heart lurched against my ribs.

'It's yourself,' he said.

He had on a navy T-shirt and his upper arms bulged with muscle. His aftershave reeked of some cheap fragrance. I thought it was disguising his body smells; some people spray themselves sooner than wash their bodies. Like Mammy, who most days didn't bother to fragrance herself up at all. Greasy hair, the sight of it made me feel nauseous. Reminded me of chip oil.

I went to pass him and he blocked my path, so quickly done – it felt as though he'd cut my very breath in two.

'What's your hurry?' he said.

His face was close to mine. I could see the yellow in the whites of his eyes. He smiled the distant cousin of a smile. It was a smile that said I could proceed after he'd finished saying what he wanted to say. I understood then that my bumping into him was no accident – he'd been watching me.

He stepped back, and though people passed us by and were in the vicinity, they probably thought nothing of us standing there – he was just a smiling man talking away to a young woman.

'You know Beth – you served her chips and chicken – served her Young Benny too.'

'I don't know what you're talking about.'

'Listen here, you. I've squeezed far thicker necks than yours, believe me – till their eyes popped out of their fucking heads.'

'What do you want?'

'Money. You've caused my Beth her fair share of worry going off with Benny like that. And I think you owe us both now.'

'Do you really think that I have money? Really?'

'I've racked up gambling debts that need paying – I owe to the Ra, the boys, you know, old friends of mine, good buddies except when it comes to owing them cash. Would be a way of making up for what you've done.'

'I've got nothing.'

'It's in your interest to make a donation.'

'I–'

'Listen, have you any idea what I used to do for a living?'

He was speaking through his clenched teeth.

'You're a mechanic.'

He said, 'I hurt people – and some people think I still do that sort of thing. I would prefer to stay in retirement, but God, some people are making that a fucking hard choice for me . . . decent people, you know . . . are prepared to do what's needed for me to take care of people, if you know what I mean.' He let that sink in and then he went on, 'And there I was, thinking it a personal matter to break someone up, for you messing with Beth's marriage – a matter of honour . . . for no monetary reward. Now I could kill two birds with one stone, couldn't I? If I was of a mind. If the price goes up, maybe I will.'

I told myself that Luigi was a fucking bollix for whinging to this creep. I gave over my last twenty quid and I knew by the silence that it was okay for me to walk on.

But it took me ages to stop shivering.

57

In the morning, after a breakfast of scrambled eggs and toast, she packs her car with her things. The five-year-old van fits all of her belongings, with space left over. She is surprised at the paucity of what she owns. But then, she had brought precious little, material-wise, into the relationship. The house, furniture, the lot, is Dan's property.

Pangs of nostalgia fly about in her tummy as she pulls out of the drive and along the avenue. The good times with Dan, the laughs, the tours and holidays, the way they seemed right for each other. But nothing lasts. Nothing ever stays the same. Things change, the past just serves to haunt us with good and bad memories.

She takes a right turn, catches a stench of skunk roadkill, and passes a man busy picking up garbage that had spilled from the back of his truck. She will miss Dan, but if she stayed, she would have to face the fact that he is, and has always been, a stranger to her. A sobering exercise for her, that realisation, this upheaval.

The beauty of the nature around her warms the cold numb feeling within her. I love October, she thinks. The last breathes of summer, the shedding of leaves, the early morning mist and fog, the drab but still and silent air, as though the season is holding its last breath, not wanting to release it, for it is its last breath, the one that allows it to treasure all of its others – to bask in memory, knowing that its time has come and will be gone with the first blow of winter.

A tear falls, another … letting go is never easy, but the seasons march on … she will be okay; she will try her best to be okay.

She'd called him several times last night, but he didn't answer. Left a message on the last attempt, to wish him well, to leave a couple of months sit between them before meeting up for a coffee – that is, if he wanted. Take care, she'd texted, I hope you sorted out what you felt needed sorting out in Ireland.

58

Roger Hall was as good as his word; he stayed away. I was sitting with Dan in the corner of the pub, next to a tall window patterned with yellow tulips. The wide sill held a row of old hardback books and towers of dog-eared magazines. Photographs of pub soccer teams and ones that are more famous ones hung on the walls. Roger sat at the counter, with his back to us, *The Daily Mirror* spread on the counter under his eyes. He glanced at me, took my smile of gratitude and gave me a sly one in return.

Everyone said hello to me – the few customers there, the bar owner, Kevin, and a part-time barman I had met briefly, who was new.

Dan said brightly, 'You're very popular.'

He had on a white shirt and navy slacks, with canvas ankle boots. He was drinking a pint of Heineken and I was on my fifth vodka – Dan thought it was my first, but I'd been drinking in the bedsit earlier, trying to numb my nerves. I'd scrubbed my teeth with mint toothpaste and gargled mint mouthwash and chewed mint gum, hoping to drown the smell of alcohol. Dan said nothing if he'd noticed, and neither did he criticise me with his eyes, which he was still prone to doing. He kept it all hidden because he wanted so badly for the evening to go well.

'I can't help it if people like me,' I smiled.

He grinned and said, 'I've got no college tomorrow.'

Indirectly, he was asking to spend the night with me. He was being so nice and I thought that maybe I should let him stay over. He'd stayed with me once before. Usually he'd be gone from the bedsit about a half an hour after we'd made love. Then, I'd go to the pub, or Roger would come up if he'd seen Dan leaving. Dan would have to promise to be quiet … silent. Because if Kevin heard us at it – I would have to remind him again – I'd be homeless. In reality, it was Roger who concerned me. He could turn menacing over very little.

'My mother – she invited us round to dinner on Sunday,' Dan said, trying to make it sound it as if it was okay if I said it was too soon.

'Really?' I said, genuinely amazed, going on to tell him about Mammy's offer.

I thought why not. There were plenty of why nots – I was just too stupid and blind to see them, more stupid than blind. A tiny part of me wanted to show him my roots, so he could walk if he wanted to – to give him something to dwell upon. There were times when I wanted to break things off, but I saw he was my chance of getting out of what would probably be a shitty life – he'd gotten me a job and he wasn't hard to put up with and I liked him, but I wasn't passionately mad about him.

His sister entered the pub and looked around. At her shoulder was a tall man, well built. I could see her nose climb and I could tell she wasn't at all happy to be here. When she saw Dan, she gave a circular wave and pushed her teeth against her lips to show a smile, though it looked more as if she was chewing on dirt.

Dan stood up and introduced us. She was thin and wore expensive clothes, more expensive than mine, but

I thought she was going to have to peel her boyfriend's eyes off me. It made me feel good. I wore my tight-fitting, light-blue sweater and grey jeans. Dan went to buy a round of drinks and Billy J., at Teresa's nod, joined him at the counter.

'I hear you're working at Folan's,' she said.

'I am.'

'And here too – you are keeping yourself busy.'

'Idle hands, yeah – what is it you work at?'

'I don't. Officially that is. Billy J. is a horse trainer and I help him with the books.'

'Oh, that's interesting – has he trained any winners?'

'A few – last year he'd twelve, and eighteen the year before. He's on the six mark this year. It's a tough business.'

'That's good, though, isn't it, to be training winners? Some trainers don't have any year in and year out and go broke.'

'Hmm, they do – and hence the worry.'

Dan brought the drinks to the table and packets of crisps and peanuts. Billy J. lit up a thin cigar and pinched his nose a couple of times, looked at the telly, though I knew it wasn't where he wanted to rest his eyes.

We chatted, all of us, but it was forced, and after about an hour, Billy J. glanced at his watch and said to Teresa, 'I've to see a horse off to Worcester.'

Teresa explained, sounding like she was used to catching his shortfall of information. 'He's a runner in England and needs to be there to make sure everything goes well.'

'Are you going to England?' Dan said to Billy J.

'Tomorrow morning. Why?'

'I'd like a duty free....'

He and Billy J. walked to the middle of the floor.

'Well, it was nice meeting you, Ena,' Teresa said.

'Same here.'

I wondered would she give me a good report to her mother. I somehow doubted it.

When they were gone, Dan relaxed; his shoulders didn't seem as high. Like me, he knew that Teresa had been scouting for their mother.

'See that old guy there – don't make it an obvious look over,' Dan said.

Roger Hall.

'What about him?'

'When I was at the counter, he was staring at the page 3 girl – and said to the barman – "your one has a fine pair of tits".'

Why is he telling me this?

'Do you know him?'

'No.'

'No?'

'He's not a regular.'

'I wouldn't like you to be serving his sort – you're too good to be doing that.'

'Am I?'

'You are and you have to start believing that you are.'

'They're just tits, Dan, paper tits – wise up.'

He said nothing.

'Don't be worrying about me; I'm well able to handle his sort,' I said, trying to fix his wounded look.

I was about to add something else when I saw Beth Foster and Young Benny come in from the snug. She shot me a poisonous look. She stormed over and threw the contents of her glass at me.

I think Dan was the only shocked person in the place.

She called me a whore and only Young Benny grabbed a hold of her; I think she would have put her glass into my face had he not. I was mortified, but I still lost my temper. I wanted to rip her eyes out, and Young Benny's too, but Dan came between us, and I was furious with him for doing that. What the fuck brought them into my pub? I'd never seen them in here before – there were loads of other pubs they could have gone into.

Dan kept staring at me in the bedsit. His mouth was open too, and the colour had fled from his face.

'What?' I snapped, taking off my clothes.

'What was that all about?'

'I don't know. How the fuck would I?'

'She said you went with her husband.'

'Do you believe her?'

'No,' he said, but he didn't know what to believe.

'She's cuckoo,' I said. 'She has it nailed into her tiny brain that something happened between me and that ugly piece of shit she's married to.'

He rubbed his lips.

I was starkers. The bitch had soaked me through.

'I need to wash,' I said. 'Fix us a drink from the press there, will you?'

He hesitated.

'Behind you,' I said, though I knew his hesitation wasn't caused by not knowing where I kept the drink, but because he thought I had downed enough. But tonight was one of those nights when enough would never be enough.

'Okay.'

After I washed, still naked, I went to change the sheets in the bed, then remembered that my spare set was in the wash. They'd have to do – I was sure Roger's sweat had long dried into them. Anyway, Dan would be on top.

'You can stay if you want,' I said.

The notion of what he was in for served to shut him up for a while.

In the morning, I woke to the shower running. Reached over to the bedside locker and checked the time on my Timex – just gone 10 a.m. My head hurt, felt as though there was a weight at the back of it, anchoring it to the pillow. Aspects of last night came back to me in an almost slide-show sequence, like out of the projector Daddy used to own. Waves of anxiety broke over my stomach, stirring the nerves there. I suddenly needed to pee. His pillow cover was patchy with blood and I had a dim memory of being awakened in the night by the sound of Dan grinding his teeth. Mammy used to say that worms caused that to happen – worms and worry.

He opened the door and the steam behind him resembled a cloud. He'd a towel wrapped around his waist. He shot me a funny look. And I thought, you bastard. Men never argue or complain until after they'd had their fill.

'Why the glum face?' I asked, padding across the floor to the bathroom.

'I don't have a glum face,' he said.

I stepped into bathroom, closed the door. For a lad that was after spending a night in bed with me, he looked, I dunno, maybe not glum – something else, though. But the word wouldn't come to me. He'd used all the hot water from the geyser and I had to make do with sponging myself. I opened the window to let out the steam and smoked while I sat on the toilet – I tried not to think of last night.

'We need to talk,' he said, the instant I was dressed.

Noble behaviour, I thought with some sarcasm, in not attacking a girl with her knickers down.

'Yes,' I said, airily, 'what about?'

He hadn't kissed me so far this morning, or been in any way affectionate. He handed me a mug of coffee. I dipped in a cube of brown sugar and stirred.

'Well?' I prompted.

'I'm not your first, am I?'

'First what?' I said.

He pulled a face that asked me not to play stupid.

'I never said I was, did I?'

He went to the window and stood with his back to me, his hands on the sill. There were spatters of bird dirt on the glass.

'I was hoping that you would have been,' he said.

'I was hoping it wouldn't have mattered to you.'

'Who?' he said, so fiercely the glass rattled in its sash frame.

'Don't you raise your voice to me.'

He whisked around and said, 'Who?'

'Oh,' I said, 'do you mean who … or with how many?'

'It's like that, is it?'

'I think that what I did before I met you is absolutely none of your business.'

This settled him a little, softened his features. What I'd said made him believe I hadn't acted out of order since we'd started going out. Part of me wanted to shout at him to get the fuck out and tell him we were done, and I thought it might have been the right thing for both of us – but some other part of me put a clamp on my tongue.

'If you're going to badger me over stuff from my past, Dan, you should go,' I said quietly.

'Okay,' he said, coming over to me.

He kissed my cheek and we hugged each other.

'Go easy,' I said, lying on the bed, tensing at the first creak of the springs.

'We didn't last night,' he said.

Oh Jesus, I thought, our loud groans, moans, squeaking bedsprings and pounding headboard rushed to my mind.

And the pleasure too – so hot. I pushed the memories of the racket away from me and kept quiet, instead biting into his neck, his shoulder, running my nails down his back. Chewed too on what Roger would say, because no doubt he would. He was like that now, always passing sharp remarks.

59

She was settled in the new apartment and happy enough
with it too. She burned sage and prayed in the four rooms
and the next day read for a man who told her that the last
time she'd read the cards for him, she said for him to get his
eyes checked out. And luckily for him that he did, because
he had a tumour behind his left eye.

'Saved my life, for sure,' he said. 'But don't tell me any
bad stuff that you see – I don't want to know. All I'm asking
you is to see if you can trace my daughter, she's been missing
for six months. Do you think you can help with that?'

And he wants me to do it without telling him bad news?

She is settled in for the evening, watching a western on TV,
when she hears the phone ringing in the hall, where she had left
it charging. She had yet to get the main line looped in.

'Hello,' she says.

No answer.

Dan, she thinks.

Might have been.

No message left.

Maybe it was him, and he couldn't bring himself to talk
– perhaps call him back?

Something is going down with him, she is sure. She feels
it – whatever he has found out has struck his heart with
tsunami force.

60

Dan wanted to stick around for a bit, and I didn't mind so much at first, but then he started to wear at me, so I said I had to get ready for work and needed a rest.

'Were you supposed to work at the pharmacy today?' he said slowly, as if he'd been cooking his words for a while.

I said, 'I've the day off.'

A lie, but I couldn't face into the expression he would pull. His talk about behaving responsibly. He didn't believe me, but he said nothing. On his way out, I asked him to do me a favour.

'Sure,' he said.

'Will you call into Kitty and tell her I'm sick, but hope to be in tomorrow?'

He nodded, smiled, but it wasn't a genuine smile, a false growth of one is all – more of a nervous tic at my sheer nerve. That I could skip work, lie to him about it, and then casually admit it, just to get him to do something for me.

He sighed and said, 'Okay.'

'Just go,' I said, smiling.

He kissed me on the lips and I said, pushing him away gently, 'Just go.'

I closed the door behind him. He knocked on it and begged for us to spend the whole day together.

'Go,' I said brightly, 'go on.'

He forced a laugh and left. I imagined him going down the stairs, shrinking in size as he went. I moved to the window and watched him walk up the street with his hands in his pockets.

To wash away my thumping headache and an anxious feeling that was tying itself into knots in my stomach, I set to cleaning the bedsit: changed the bed linen, washed the windows, including the sill where patches of mould were black islands in a sea of white gloss. I lit a lavender-scented candle and opened the top windows to let the breeze in. I wanted the smell of sweaty men out of my space.

I borrowed the communal hoover from Kevin, who was stocktaking in the bar. He said nothing about last night, though I sensed he wanted to say something, to lay blame at my feet, but in the end, he focused on counting his bottles of Babycham, pointing with his pen in the direction of the Nilfisk.

I lay on the bed for an hour, read some of the poems from a book written by long-dead poets, which Dan had given me as a present. I didn't like many of them. They were mostly written by men, who had no idea of what it was really like to be a woman in a world ruled by men. This morning, I thought, was a perfect example – Kevin had looked at me as though I was dirt his Nilfisk had passed by. Beth was in the wrong, completely, to have attacked me, and maybe he would give her a dirty look too, if he saw her this afternoon. Probably not, though. He would consider her the wronged wife, entitled to exact vengeance for my having stolen her husband. One thing was for sure – Kevin would think nothing ill of Young Benny – sure, a man is ruled by his tool and women know this and therefore shouldn't be putting themselves in harm's way. The book was lying on my belly and I swept it to one side with my hand, knowing I'd never read another word in it – I'd told Dan, when he asked if I liked reading, that I did. But I'd meant Enid Blyton and other easy reading, not stuff that'd burn out the wires in my head.

The knock on the door startled me – it was loud – and the voice came a moment after.

'Ena? I know you're in there.'

Roger.

I got up and let him in. He smelt of forest, oil and wood shavings, lines of dirt under his fingernails. Usually he kept himself relatively spick and span. He was wearing a short-sleeved shirt – the veins in his arms resembled thick electrical wiring. In comparison, Dan's veins lay deep underground. I shouldn't compare; Dan was fifteen years younger than Roger and in terms of who was nicer, he was the easy winner.

He went to the window, pinched the netted curtain aside, and looked down at the stream of traffic. He closed the windows, said it was chilly. Picked up the book, read the title, and put it on the sill.

'Take off your clothes,' he said with ice-cold clarity.

'What?'

'Do what you're told.'

'Roger, what the fuck are you playing at?'

'Are you deaf?'

'I'll scream.'

He blocked the way to the door.

'You won't,' he said.

'I'm on my period.'

'Don't lie. Undress.'

'This is rape, you know that, don't you. It's rape and–'

'Shut it.'

'Roger, please, not like this. What's come into you?'

He was different, in his eyes. A look, a sparkle. He was menacing. Fear. I suddenly felt very, very frightened, and shook a little. I genuinely began to believe there was a strong possibility I was in danger of being killed.

'Everything,' he said, 'off. Now.'

I slipped off my clothes, quickly, and stood before him, one hand covering my breasts and the other the vee. He approached me with fierce intent, put the tip of his forefinger to the middle of my forehead and pushed me onto the bed.

After he was gone, I lay there, feeling him run out of me, feeling the pain in my arms, my legs, my neck, which he had pinched when I'd bucked against his coming inside me. He'd said nothing, just fixed his trousers and left the room, his usual twenty-pound note lying on the bedside locker. I stared for an age at the ceiling, tears spilling, trying to sort out my thoughts.

Then I got up and showered, looked at the bruises and bite he'd sown into my neck – he, who had turned 'turk' a while back for nibbling on his neck, had branded me. Given me something else to hide.

I drank half a bottle of vodka, got in under the blankets, and wished hard to be dead.

61

After leaving Teresa's place, taking a cab back to town, Dan visits the gardens, still totally in shock at what his sister has told him.

He sat at the same veranda table as before, when Irene was with him. Looked at the espresso he had bought, though he had no thirst. Here, he thought, is better than the loneliness and gloom of the B&B – here with the birdsong, foreign chatter, the greedy chaffinch, the occasional eruption of horse whinny, the raucous ducks....

He plays Teresa's words over in his head.

'So, I'll tell you,' she'd said, 'what I know – what I was told – what was confessed to me. I doubt if you'll believe me....'

She gazed at him and continued, 'Mam told me on her deathbed that she was responsible for Ena's death.'

The silence between them hung on an invisible thread of disbelief. Several times he went to speak, but his lips moved wordlessly.

'No,' he'd said, almost inaudibly.

'I've told you exactly what she told me – she said she was responsible.'

'How responsible? I mean, what the fuck does that mean?'

'That's all she said. I think she might have meant she felt guilty for being so nasty towards her.'

Silence.

'That's all she said, Dan. It could also be that she meant much more.'

He concentrates hard, summoning old memories to lend them a fresh perspective – Mam had died almost six weeks to the day after Ena's murder. Her health had rapidly gone downhill, but it hadn't been good for some years, since Dad's passing. He used to feel guilty – she'd been so angry and upset at his involvement with Ena and had pretty much cut him out of her life. Now, it seems she'd slipped and drowned in her own well of sorrow.

What had she meant by saying that word 'responsible'?

Was it she who had hit Ena with the brick?

Hardly.

She would have to walk a mile out of town, in the dead hours, a cold starless night. He doesn't see that strength or determination in her. It's not impossible, but it is, he considers, highly improbable.

'Did you believe her?' he asked Teresa.

'Yes – otherwise, I don't think she would have said it on her deathbed – she knew she was dying. If she had more to tell me, she didn't get the chance.'

'Why didn't you tell me this before?'

Silence.

'It would have taken me off the list of suspects a lot earlier, don't you think?'

Still, no response.

'It doesn't make sense – why would you provide an alibi for Billy J., knowing what you knew? Why didn't you tell the guards?'

'Billy J. was a different scenario. You? Why do you think they stopped bringing you in for questioning?'

The heat came off so suddenly, he remembered – the relief was huge, a little scary. It was like waiting for an avalanche to come roaring.

She had kept staring at him, trying to pull a realisation from him, like a fisherman would reel in a large pike.

His mother....

62

Dan said it was good planning to get both visits to our mothers over and done with on the same day. I wasn't really listening to him. I was very sore, after what Roger Hall had done two days earlier, and no amount of showers left me feeling clean.

'Are you okay?' he said, as we walked along the narrow footpath, past Luigi's.

'Yeah, I'm all right. You?'

'I can understand you being a little nervous.'

'About?'

He nudged me with his elbow and said, 'Meeting the feared Molly Somers.'

All I knew of his mother was that she was a big woman with a big husky voice she used to great effect at town meetings; the sort who knew how not to let someone get a word in edgeways.

'I'm not worried about her,' I said.

'Then what is it? What's bothering you, Ena?'

'Nothing.'

'Don't say nothing, when I know it's something. Are you not feeling well or something?'

'Jesus,' I said, 'do you want me to make up stuff?'

'The row wasn't your fault.'

It took moments to register with me that he was talking about Beth and her attack. I said nothing, so he would think he had my problem figured and wouldn't keep trying to lance the truth from me.

A mild day with not much cloud, what cloud there was, was white – it felt like black cloud shadowed my heart. His mother's house – God, the garden. You could have built five of Mammy's type of house on it. And full of small trees, shrubs and flowers. I felt shame rising within me: a couple of hours from now, I'd be walking into Mammy's and Dan would be feeling and thinking the opposite of what I was right now. One family owns all of this?

Fuck me.

How is it that possible? How is it fair?

He brought me around the back, and the back yard was long and an extension of the front – it looked like the Garden of Eden, I thought. There were two green wooden sheds at the end of it and a glasshouse to the left. A man was tinkering with a car, leaning in and out from under the bonnet. I couldn't put a name to his face. He looked at us, gave a wave. Dan said he was his mother's mechanic cum gardener – Owen Noctor. Him! I felt a chill blow across me. Then I got angry.

'That's that cow's father,' I said, thinking of Beth.

'Shush,' Dan said, 'it's not his fault she's like that.'

He went through a small conservatory, into a large kitchen. I smelt apple tarts cooking in the range. I heard her coming down the hall, calling, 'Dan….'

In she came, a tornado. Her hair was grey and styled, a blue rinse shot through it. She wore a white blouse and long yellow skirt. She'd just applied coconut moisturiser and her fleshy oval face gleamed. Dan had her eyes; there was that same way of looking at someone that I likened to a gravedigger poking at hard earth, loosening the soil so he could begin digging proper.

We shook hands. She noticed right off that I had a wart on my right thumb and recommended a good lotion. It was a wart I had hardly noticed myself, and here she was catching it in the net cast by her eyes.

'It must be in stock in Kitty's,' she said, ushering me to the table.

'I'll look,' I said, pulling out a chair. It was heavy. A sign of good timber and expense.

The table was set for dinner.

'I hope you like chicken?" she said.

'I do, yes. Can I give you a hand with anything?'

'Not at all, sit down – Dan, will you get the drinks?'

The good cutlery was out, silver with a lovely pearl handle. Red napkins.

Dan got bottles of red lemonade and orange from the fridge. He asked his mother about Teresa and Billy J., if she'd heard from them, and his mother said she'd been talking to them only that morning.

As if to make a point, she hardened her tone a little and added, 'They won't be joining us.'

I took two meanings from that: either she'd had cross words with them, or someone had filled her in on the row in Kevin's pub and told her what Beth had screamed about me being a whore. Which I was, when I thought on it – it's what Roger thought, with his twenty quid lying on the bedside locker after he'd shagged me. That's the word he used, I didn't like it. I used to think the money was a helping hand sort of thing – he knew how strapped I was for cash, and he did stand up for me when Kevin hiked the rent that time. I'd liked him and thought he was okay, but now…. He left me feeling very sore in soul and both holes. Like a rabbit on a spit.

She gave me a breast and Dan a leg and said Grace before meals. There was a photograph of the family on a small lace-covered table in a corner and another of Dan's father, I took it to be, because a votive candle was burning in front of it. A nice respectful thing that. He mustn't have been like my own father, a man with two wives and children on separate islands.

'So, Ena, tell me this,' she said. 'How are you getting on in Kitty's?'

'I love it, Mrs Somers.'

'And Frieda?'

'She's nice too.'

'She's my best friend – you won't come across a more solid and a dependable woman. When my Jack died, she was an absolute godsend to have around, wasn't she, Dan?'

'Yes.'

'She'd do anything for you, but if you're unfortunate to get on her wrong side, watch out – she knows how to hold a grudge like no other person I know.'

I looked at Dan, he winked with the eye she couldn't see.

'And you're working in a bar too, I hear,' she said, staring at the bones of her chicken.

'It pays the rent,' I said evenly, but with a sinking feeling.

'You don't live at home?'

A question she knew the answer to, which put a sizzle of resentment into my blood.

'Mammy and I, we don't get along,' I said.

'Isn't that a shame,' she said, looking directly at me.

I shrugged. I'd no appetite and it was killing me to eat the chicken. Bursting for a pee too. I was going to have to ask.

'Of course,' she said, 'there's one on the landing and another off the hall.'

The loo was bigger than my bedroom in Mammy's house. The walls were tiled blue and white and the floor was a cold, shiny grey – I imagined it was solidified rain. A bar of pink soap lay in a seashell-shaped dish, and the toilet paper was soft and thick to feel. I dug a small mirror out of my shoulder bag and used it to have a good look at my fanny. I thought I needed stitching, but it was okay … ish. My arse wasn't … but maybe that would stop bleeding in a day or two. I'd wait till then. Then I would go to the doctor, I promised myself, if it hadn't.

'Dessert?' Mrs Somers said, after I'd re-entered the kitchen.

Before I replied, she said, 'We've got lemon cheesecake and chocolate fudge cake.'

'A slice of cheesecake,' I said, 'a thin slice, please.'

'Have to mind the figure – you've got such a lovely figure. I used to be so thin too. I'd love to be thin again,' she paused. 'Dan, get the cream will you?'

I'd say truth be known she hadn't been thin a day in her life, at least not the sort of thinness she was making out.

When Dan left the kitchen, she began to grill me. About Mammy, Daddy, my hopes for the future, then going on to say what a great career Dan had in front of him.

She kept on at it when Dan rejoined us, wrapping what she really wanted to say in layers of nonsense chat. Primarily, I was not to wreck her son's professional career. Not even hinder it.

She was placing that charge at me too, unspoken. I was taking his mind off his studies. She also mentioned an ex-girlfriend of his, who had recently won a beauty competition and was heading to London on an academic scholarship. On and on she went, rubbing my nose in it.

Dan grew uncomfortable, because she wouldn't let up trying to make me feel small and insignificant, sticking the knife in by making it clear that he could have done much better for himself than me.

She was right, without doubt, he did deserve better. But *he* wanted *me*.

'Did you do your Leaving Cert, Ena?' she asked, while pouring coffee.

'No,' I said. 'I didn't like studying.'

She knows I didn't … why ask?

Molly showed her dismay by furrowing her brow.

'A good education is paramount to a successful working career,' she said.

'I agree,' I said. 'I might go back and study for it – I'm still young enough. I was moved up a grade because I was very bright.'

'Really?' she said, a little impressed.

'Hmm,' I said, finishing off the cheesecake.

I was bullshitting her, of course.

On the way to Mammy's, Dan apologised for his mother's behaviour.

'She thinks you should go to London after Donna,' I said.

'I'm not interested in her.'

'Or she's not interested in you.'

'We're not interested in each other.'

'Your mother doesn't like me,' I said.

'She does.'

'No.'

'She's like that with everyone.'

'With all your other girlfriends?'

'You're the first one I brought home.'

'Apart from Donna?'

'She wasn't a girlfriend – we're more like cousins, if you follow, we've known each other for years.'

I began to grow increasingly conscious of where we were going: it had seriously dawned on me for the first time. I fretted. The estates we passed seemed dour and squashed up in comparison to his detached house. And my estate was the largest in town, a council mish-mash of houses, row upon row, each as poor-looking as the next. They were homes though, good or bad. Homes.

While I had been apprehensive about visiting his mother – I hadn't, till we got close to Mammy's, realised that I would be doubly apprehensive at bringing Dan to the house in which I was reared. He was bound to have some of his mother in him, and that wasn't his fault, it was a fact. It bothered me very much what he would think. Before now, if he'd ended things with me, I wouldn't have minded – and I'd been thinking of ending it too. I didn't think he mattered much in the scheme of things, but now I was less sure. I saw how things could be for me, with him. I could grow to love him, couldn't I? If we did marry – I'd be able to flash the middle finger in the face of the town. I wouldn't have to work. I could mind house and cook dinners and have nice little kids and not have to worry about money or dirty fuckers coming to poke me.

'I think we should leave Mammy's for another time,' I said.

'It wouldn't be fair on her,' he said.

'I suppose not.'

'What are you worried about?'

'It's far from Buckingham Palace.'

'So.'

'Mammy is far from being a queen.'

'Here … that doesn't matter.'

Deep into the heart of the estate we went, through an alleyway, between backyards blooming with full clotheslines

– a couple spat bad language at each other, a dog arched its spine and shat, kids went by on tricycles.

I knocked on the front door. And again. Peered through the frosted glass into the hall. Then the door opened.

Mammy stood there with a cigarette in the corner of her mouth. She had on a sky-blue cardigan and a long red skirt, food-stained.

'Jesus,' she said, 'this is a surprise – come along in, come in.'

She walked ahead of us into the kitchen, saying she'd put the kettle on. The place was awash with loose clothes and bags of them – her wine-coloured sewing machine stood in the middle of the floor.

'Mammy,' I said, 'you invited us down.'

'Did I?' she said, tipping her fag ash into the sink. 'I must be losing my marbles altogether.'

It felt like someone was putting the squeeze on my stomach.

'Clear off some of the clothes and sit down,' she said. 'It doesn't take long to make tea and fix a sandwich.'

'We've eaten,' I said.

'This is Dan, is it?' she said.

'Dan Somers,' Dan said, taking her hand and shaking it.

'A proper gentleman, like your dad.'

'You knew him?'

'Everyone did.'

'Mammy?'

'Get the cups, Ena – you're not a stranger here – you know where everything is.'

She'd forgotten about us coming down. And didn't care an iota about the forgetting. For the first time I saw the question form on Dan's face, 'What the hell am I letting myself in for?'

She spoke above the rising boil of the kettle, telling us that my brother and sister had gone to England with Josie. Dan asked the question with a lift of an eyebrow, and I said they lived with their aunts. He never asked why they weren't living at home. Mammy said they were better off, and so was she. The look on Dan's face – it was as though he were looking at a gorilla in a cage, with the bars slowly disappearing in front of his eyes, and danger gradually presenting itself.

63

He had tried again to call Irene. Failed to connect. He'd wanted her insight, her advice, otherworldly or whatever, about the things he had heard and what he should do about them. Is Teresa spoofing? If so, why? Mam isn't around to contest what Teresa had said. Isn't it possible for Teresa to have concocted this story? To keep Billy J. in the clear, or perhaps she herself had been involved in the killing?

He no longer knows what to believe. He'd been snatching at a straw in the wind, thinking that Billy J. was the killer. Ena hadn't liked him – she'd said he gave her the creeps – he was the only man he had heard her say that about. Yet, she'd slept with him. Paranoia, though, is what he went by in sussing Billy J. as the killer. His brush with death ignited this raging quest within him, but it had always been there, buried in the cave of his soul, because he had left Ireland to get away from accusing eyes, the whispers, the voice pitched above a whisper so he would hear and question himself if he had heard correctly, the moment passing for him to retort. He went to the States as a young man, one who did not feel like an immigrant, more someone who'd been banished, excommunicated.

With the passage of time the tiny flame lessened. He focused on creating a new life, but the burning within him always pulsed, if faintly. That flickering torch of injustice perpetuated against himself and Ena. An innocent man, a murdered woman.

He needed it sorted, and ignored the statement that came to him in a voice that did not remotely resemble his: you'll not see justice this side of life.

Suspects had died since the murder – Luigi, he had learned; Benny Foster, whose wife had assaulted Ena in the pub; Han Kelly (not a suspect but someone who might know things); the others … Poncho McDonagh, who'd found her broken body; Roger Hall. People he had asked about them, their whereabouts, had never heard of their names, others knew but played dumb. Others simply did not want to discuss the matter, fobbing him off with trite comments such as 'I knew him … but I couldn't tell you where he's living now … he might have a brother in….'

The pub in which Ena had worked for a while had changed ownership several times, and her old bedsit is now a storeroom. Don Lally. Mirror Mickey. Others? He can't recall – he is facing into a blank wall.

Maurice Smith is coming in to see him, off sick leave. It had been worthwhile making that initial call to the station – he had almost decided not to bother, but instead to call in when he'd arrived in Ireland. He would have felt awkward introducing himself to those who'd be strangers to the case – for no doubt the faces would be new and young and strange. Puzzled expressions – the widower of a murdered woman, a suspect, after decades, home to do what exactly? Seek justice?

Maurice shakes his hand in the station's reception area. He's in mufti; navy slacks, a worn combat jacket. Along the corridors, taking two lefts and a right, Maurice mentions that he is head to toe arthritic, soon to be pensioned off.

Dipping his voice low, half smiling, he says that he can't wait to be home every day, struggling to screw the top off a milk carton and suchlike.

'Don't mind my talking so much – the missus says she got unlucky in that the arthritis doesn't affect my mouth.'

A gruff man, with bushy eyebrows – a bit of a character here, Dan suspects – someone neither afraid of nor too respectful of higher authority, perhaps emboldened by age and his experiences. A man who could handle himself, who had information on people, information people would prefer others never to find out. He must have an arsenal of leverages.

In a room with wall-to-wall filing cabinets looking at a small square table and two grey polyproplene chairs, Maurice listens to him. Into the silence he tells him quite bluntly that Dan's wife was the first murder victim he had seen – unfortunately, it would not be his last.

'A few others since then,' he says, 'averaging one every five years. I wish it were one every twenty.'

Dan waits for him to say something else.

The guard says, 'Well, my memory on your late wife's case is sketchy, but after you made the appointment to meet with me, I went and looked up….'

He opens a box file and retrieves a green folder. 'The case – we kept it open – officially that is. Unofficially, it's been closed a long time, and perhaps time has caught up with the perp – we have no way of knowing. This is the only unsolved murder on our books.'

'I remember being told by Detective Carey that–'

'Ah, Billy, he passed away about five years ago. Decent man.'

'That the forensic report stated that it was, in all probability, a left-handed person who'd hit Ena with the brick.'

'Probably isn't a certainty.'

'I know.'

'The lads hauled in everyone who knew her and questioned them at length – they brought some back for further questioning. I sat in for some of the interviews.'

'Me, my brother-in-law, my sister, my mother....'

'Yes,' Smith says, index finger moving down the list in the file. 'I remember you. I remember ...' the last word falling kindly.

Dan says, 'The killer's name is in there, do you think?'

Smith shrugs, 'Who's to say? Luigi O'Malley is dead. Roger Hall, dead. Don Lally, dead. Billy J.,' he cocked his wild eyebrow, 'your brother-in-law, your sister, you, Benny Foster, dead. His widow, Beth, alive, I think – at least she was the last time I saw her. Suspects all.'

'I was easily a prime suspect.'

'Until your sister told us about her mother's supposed deathbed confession.'

'You don't believe her?'

'Let's say I wouldn't have an opinion formed.'

'So....'

'My thoughts?'

'Yes.'

He sighs, 'It's not easy – take Roger Hall – you would think he was a perfect fit for the murder, but he was with someone else that night – his story held up. Don Lally – no – my money wouldn't be on him. Luigi, yeah ... maybe ... but, so too your sister and brother-in-law, and it could be she's telling the truth. Your mother, Molly, was someone on the interview list, but she wasn't got to before she passed....'

'And it could be a stranger,' Dan suggested, wondering if the sergeant would mind if he sifted through the material in the box.

'Or three.'

'Pardon?'

Three?

'Three, three sets of foot imprints were found at the scene – they were photographed. We lifted three plaster casts of footprints, but nothing came from it. We know one pair belonged to Ena.'

'Male or female shoes?'

'Couldn't be determined.'

'I–'

'I'm going to give you a few minutes to look through the stuff, okay? I should warn you, though, there are a couple of photo albums that won't be easy for your eyes. Do you follow?'

'Yes, thanks.'

'So, I'll leave you to it.'

'I appreciate this.'

'Well, thirty-one years is a long wait. It's a historical case now. I'm not sure anything you find is going to help you sleep easier at night – but I'm not going to be a wind pushing against you. The price is that if you square something, you let me be the first to know. Deal?'

A silence fills the room; it seems to suck away the air and energy.

He puts his hand into the box and removes a ream of paper. He places it beside the green file. He takes out his mobile phone and turns the camera on, ready to snap in the event of something catching his eye.

His phone rings. In his hand, it rings....

Private number.

'Hello?' he says.

'Hi, Dan.'

'Irene.'

'This is a quick call.'

'Can I ring you later – I'm in the middle of something pretty serious right now – say in half an hour?

A pause.

'O … kay,' she says.

He picks up on her hesitancy, the reluctance to agree.

He says, 'Is it too much of an ask?'

'No,' she says, 'in half an hour.'

64

'Where are you?' Dan says, immediately after he gets through.

His tone is strained.

'Where do you think?'

'At home?'

She allows the question to settle for a second before saying, 'I moved out, Dan, we discussed this.'

'Jesus.'

'What?'

'Discuss? I discussed nothing. You didn't delay, did you? It takes you longer to decide what to have for breakfast.'

'Dan. You put the accelerator to the floor with your antics in Ireland.'

He sighs for what seems an age. Low and mournful.

He says, and she picks up on his pain, 'I thought this would blow over ... we could work it out. I just ... the whole thing took over – it's like a fire got out of control, but I'm so close ... so close....'

'Really – is that what you really thought? It would blow over? Really, Dan?'

'I was bothered, I....'

'You let your past consume your present and future.'

'How Dalai Lama of you....'

'Dan, don't.'

'So why did you call?'

She tells him about finding a book of his, *Doctor Zhivago*. It had fallen at her feet from the shelf in his study.

'What's the significance in that?' he says.

'Well, how many copies of a book have fallen at your feet, Dan?'

With deep sarcasm he says, 'Which is supposed to mean?'

'You sound worried.'

'*Doctor Zhivago* … Ena loved the film, I bought her the book, but she wasn't a big reader.'

'Can you remember what you wrote inside the cover?'

'Of course,' he says reluctantly

'Say it.'

'Irene.'

'Dan.'

'To my first and eternal love.'

'That's not me. And it's still a truism.'

'I found something out.'

'I'm not finished.'

'Go on.'

'It's time for you to stop the quest. That's what I'm taking out of this and the card reading I did for you a couple of days ago.'

'For me, in my absence?'

'Oh, I had the book present, so you were both there.'

She knows he wants to scream. She feels he is reining in his tongue.

'I'm almost … I feel it.…'

'Back away, Dan. Your health.…'

'I—'

'I'll tell you what I see, will I?'

'Do go on,' he says.

'She wants you to get on with your life. She never loved you – you were a way out of a mess for her, a rung on the ladder. You've carried the torch for far too long.'

'Listen, Irene, we were husband and wife, and someone killed my wife.'

'You think you know who did it.'

'No. I do … yes. I do know,' he says.

'Dan?'

'What?'

'It's going to crack your heart constantly whenever you think on how far down the road you've come, and have nothing to show for it.'

'You were always good at painting black.'

'It's not who you think it is.'

'If you know, spit it out.'

'It didn't come – it won't ever come.'

Silence.

'You're wrong, dead fucking wrong.'

65

He throws his mobile phone onto the bed. She had called to caution him. He had wanted to talk about his visit to the police, discuss the documents lying on his bed, but she didn't give him the angle. Because she is doing what she wants him to do, move on. The things he has learned. He has notes he'd scribbled, three statements he'd pocketed, a quick selection. Knew he shouldn't have, that it was a betrayal of trust, but if he had asked for copies ... not a hope. He was told that, in all but word.

The Final Investigation Report. He reads the concluding paragraph. The language is old-world cop: 'To date, no one has been found guilty of this crime. Should further information come to light, a report will be submitted.'

An official admission that the murder inquiry was unsolved and likely to remain so, yet the lid was left off a little – just a little – in the event of a sea change.

Yet of the three statements he'd plundered, one contains an explosive piece of information.

Why wasn't it spotted by the collator? Surely he or his supervisor, the superintendent who signed off on the report, would have wanted the sighting of a car in the vicinity at the time of the murder checked out? Perhaps there'd been an innocuous reason for its presence, he supposes. But if the car was mentioned in a witness statement ... of course, a drunk had seen it. A drunk is not a reliable witness, he supposes.

He pours a whiskey, the photos of the scene alive and throbbing in his mind – an apron of wet earth, muddied imprints from human footwear. Ena's, no doubt, and her murderer/s. Across the road lies a mound of red bricks outside the front garden wall of a house undergoing renovation.

She had come from there – and the man whose bed she had left said he hadn't heard a thing. No commotion, no cry for help or alarm. In his statement, he says his bedroom was at the back of the house, and he had been drinking, watching TV, and dosing off. The man admitted she had been with him. It had been an ongoing thing, on and off for a year. This man, Kevin Farrell, owned the pub, which changed names a lot. At the time, it was called The Brophy Arms, the place where Ena had worked and lived above.

She wore no jacket. When asked why she would leave it behind in his house, on a drizzly night, Farrell said, 'I have no idea.'

He had nothing to hide, he said. Were they alone in the house all evening? No, they had guests. It was a house party for his birthday. But he insisted that everyone had been long gone before Ena set off. No, he replied to a question, he wasn't one hundred per cent sure everyone had left – he was out of it. The last question he had no answer to: 'I have no idea why she took off into the night at that hour ... I can't help you there, I'm sorry. I wish I could.'

Farrell was certain about the names of some of his guests, a couple of members of staff, past and present, likewise concerning those who rented his bedsits, friends. His brother who left because they had words. Others he is certain were in the pub, but could not swear if they had come down to his house after closing time. It was about 3 a.m. when they drifted away from his home place. He was too well-oiled to have a full recollection – they would have to ask around.

Why didn't he remain on in the pub, have the party behind closed doors? He said there were tinkers parked close to his house and he was afraid they'd break in or steal from his yard – stuff needed for doing up the house. They'd already lifted stuff; a few nights before the party he'd found bricks and a bag of burst cement across from the house.

The names were crosschecked. Roger Hall, Young Benny Foster, Luigi O'Malley, were confirmed as being in the house, all said they left together, with Luigi admitting he had driven home under the influence of alcohol. The innocuous detail missed: Roger Hall said Beth Foster was in the pub, and had been in Kevin's house later on. In her statement, Beth said she wasn't in the house, but had dropped her husband there.

That, Dan thinks, does not make sense: she gave a lift to her husband and left him at a house where she knew Ena would be – a woman she'd attacked for having an affair with her husband. Hardly – so why wasn't this mentioned in the police report? Roger Hall, was he lying about Beth being in the house or was it a genuine error on his part? He is the only witness who put her there.

Luigi stated that there'd been a blue car, maybe a Ford Cortina, parked up the road from the house – he had seen it as he passed it by; remembered because his heart had given such a high jump – he had thought it was the police. None of the others saw this car, or if they had, they had kept it to themselves. A call to Smith revealed the blue car was traced to a taxi driver in town.

Unless there was another....

The car ... the one his mother intended to give him for his birthday – because of this detail, the certainty of it being blue, Dan understands the truth of what happened on that dark murky night. It slices across his being, leaving his hands shaking. Sinks like a blade into his heart too. The impact of his mother's involvement sickens him to the centre of his soul. Jesus, how the fuck could she? And yet, he has a small understanding of why she would – and this causes him to retch.

66

In the weeks following the visit to Mammy's, I started to get in trouble at the chemist. Kitty Folan married her Australian boyfriend and went off on a prolonged honeymoon for six months. Lucky thing. He was nothing to look at and neither was she. I wasn't invited to the wedding, none of us staff were, but we still chipped in and bought her a present. Her sister, Frieda, changed the shift roster, which was merely a swapping around of our days, just to leave us in no doubt who was calling the shots. Her attitude to me before the visit to Dan's mother was one of cold indifference – tolerating me, like I was a bad crack in the wall that needed sorting, but she had to hold off until the right time for the fixing.

'If you don't like it,' she said to us in the kitchen before we opened up after lunch, 'you know where the door is.'

As the others left the room, she said, 'Ena, a word.'

She was Hitler with tits. Her large frame blocked the window. Her cheeks hung loose, and the lines across her forehead ran even and deep. She always had a disapproving look. It was easy to see how she could be friends with Dan's mother: they must have been cut from the same cloth.

I said nothing.

'It was brought to my attention that you are taking those disgusting things out of the bin.'

She threw me with this revelation.

'What things?' I said, buying time, trying to think who could have swung me.

'The con-doms,' she said.

The way she said the word, breaking it in two, well … wouldn't be good for a condom user if that were to happen.

'But they were thrown out,' I said, 'you won't dispense them on prescription.'

'So that no one – and that includes you – would use them.'

'Kitty does….'

'She's not here. And I'm in charge.'

If her eyes were daggers, I'd have been cut to ribbons.

'It's not to happen again.'

'There was only twenty-five in the box,' I said.

She shook her head as if what I'd said was a bothersome fly and said, 'What does that mean?'

Somewhere along my way, I'd lost the gift of knowing when to keep my mouth shut.

'I've almost run out.'

Her jaw fell, and I fled before she picked it up.

But she said later, 'You're on a formal warning.'

Said in front of a customer too, another of her friends. Like all good Catholics, they weren't happy unless they were nailing someone to the cross.

I couldn't figure out if Dan was cooling on me. He had gone quiet and silent. When I'd ask if he'd anything on his mind, he'd say there wasn't. If I pressed, he'd say he was finding his studies hard. A lie. I got it out of him eventually – his mother was giving him grief over me.

She wanted him to end the relationship.

We were in the park. An old guy was kicking an orange ball about and his small dog was running after it, sinking its teeth in and carrying it back to his owner. Some lads were hurling and punting balls over tall, crooked goalposts.

A train gathered pace and I wished I was a passenger – the train had the colours of a tiger. I liked tigers. If I died and had to come back to shithole earth, I would want to be a tiger. When I'd told Dan this last week, he said, 'You'd be a right big pussy then.' He talked a lot of shite when he had cider in him.

'Why she is giving you a hard time?' I said, a stupid question, because I knew the answer.

His face filled with pain.

'I told you,' I said, 'that she didn't like me.'

'It's just….'

'Just what?'

'She said you weren't good for me, that you were doing the dirt on me.'

'She said that?'

'Yes.'

'What do you think?'

'You know what I think.'

'You said you loved me.'

'I did say it, yes,' he said.

He looked away, watched someone reeling in a kite.

I had a ball of anger inside me. I could picture it – orange with teeth sunk into it.

I said, pinching his arm, 'We should get married … I'm pregnant.'

Tell your mother that!

Such a look of terror seized his puss, I almost said I was kidding him. Almost.

I had to get away from the bedsit, because of Roger Hall and what he might do again, so I moved back in with Mammy. She didn't mind, because she knew I'd be moving out soon enough. I'd told her that, just to get her to let me back into the house. I kept the job up in the pub and got really friendly with Kevin. I thought he'd be mad when I told him I was leaving.

He'd have to pay me the wages he was part docking in lieu of my rent.

I was walking around silently screaming in terror that Roger Hall would rape me again, because that's what he had done, and I'd healed up okay, except in my head sometimes. He'd apologised, then said I deserved it, then apologised for it again. I think he was trying to say he was sorry but that he had to be the one to teach me a lesson. Or something along those lines.

For the first time since we started going out together, I was having sex with no one only Dan. I was pregnant and felt dirty in myself.

I felt good and bad about it – good in that I didn't feel messed around or was messing him around – bad because he was usually done and dusted with me in less than two minutes, and I wanted to go for a lot longer. Older and more experienced men usually could bring me that far. Maybe he would improve in time, but I wasn't too sure. He didn't seem to stop and consider that I'd like to come too – he thought his hand to me afterwards was enough and sometimes it was.

We were out for a meal in the Chinese restaurant, finishing off a dessert of banana fritters, when he said, 'Mam's invited us down to dinner this Sunday.'

Right off, I thought my spine was going to freeze over, crack and then splinter into shards of bone.

'I can't,' I said, 'not this Sunday.'

'Okay,' he said, putting his lips to his glass of lager.

'No, I promised Mammy I'd help her with something.'

'All right,' he said.

I told him about Frieda giving me a hard time over the johnnies and he said she was real old school about such matters.

'Maybe,' I said, 'but she made out that I was stealing them, and how can you steal something that's been thrown out?'

'And you'd like me to ask Mam to have a word with her about being hard on you?'

'I think she could sack me. I think she's thinking about doing it.'

'No, Frieda's okay – she's had a tough time in the last couple of years with her son dying and her husband leaving her for another woman.'

'News to me. But she's not okay – she's a war wagon.'

'How does a person cheat on someone and live with it afterwards – like meet their wife or husband or whoever, and behave normally. How?'

There was someone spitting poison into his ear. I wanted to say that it's instinct for some people to take what's not theirs. In a way, it's not their fault. We're fucked from the start – I remember thinking that after reading in the Old Testament a passage I'd chanced upon when flipping through the pages in a shed at the back of the pub, where Kevin stored things. This man's two daughters got their father drunk on wine so as to have sex with him and get pregnant. How could we be anything other than fucked up, the lot of us – blame the ancestors, blame God even. I never turned another page in that Bible. Most people in court don't know what's between the covers they're swearing upon.

'I have no idea,' I said, looking at the last spoon of dessert in my bowl, 'but tell me this, did you tell your mother she was going to be a grandmother?

67

The solicitor contacts him to say the house has been sold, and there is nothing to keep Dan and his sister in the country. The proceeds of the sale should hit their account in about six weeks, and he will email them both the breakdown of fees incurred in its sale. Granting the solicitor power of attorney status had cut down on the need to visit the solicitor's office. Dan had agreed to a fifty-fifty split with Teresa – he regarded the worry he had caused her about chasing her for the years of half rent due to him as punishment enough.

His bags are packed and sitting on the bed. His second whiskey of the afternoon in his hand, he thinks about his visit to the murder scene that morning. Kevin's house is still standing, though he himself had stopped standing ten years after Ena's murder. Dan isn't certain of the exact spot where Ena was found. It could have been fifteen or maybe twenty yards either side of where he'd thought – time distorts the memory. But yes, certainly, thereabouts, close enough. It had been his second-last place to visit. He had finally decided on his list.

He drinks his whiskey and wonders at what she will say, her response after he tells her she can talk to him or to the police. Her call.

68

I really did get pregnant; I wasn't lying to Dan. Panic set in. I didn't know whose it was – Dan's or Roger's or Kevin's or this other man who was really good looking and had stopped in the bar one night – he was English. So, I went running; I ran for miles. I stopped, walked, and got going again, running … running … I starved myself … it didn't have a chance, not with me. I was thinking I might have to go to England, maybe ask Roger for the money, and tell him it was his. I couldn't tap Dan for money – I couldn't do that to him – I should have done, but I wasn't thinking straight or crooked. Kevin was another possibility for a fare, but he had a cold and dark face whenever money was discussed. He left no money on the locker after we'd had sex, and he behaved as if he was doing me a favour. But I could tell him I'd squeal about us to his wife, who was in Cork looking after her dying mother, and that would make him cough up. Though he might not have – he had steel. I wasn't sure which way he would turn.

Anyway, it didn't grow; the weeds in my heart choked it to death. Part of me was sad and part of me was glad – there was a part in-between too, that didn't care either way. Around about then, I told Dan that I thought I was a hundred per cent sure that I was in love with him.

He didn't say it back. He just looked at me as if he'd won the Sweeps. But I was wrong about his expression – he told me later he was disappointed I'd used the word 'thought'.

69

He walked by the house several times, rehearsing in his mind what he would say. The estate was new, middle-class, cobble-stoned driveway, in-year cars or close to it. A few saplings on the green didn't look like they were going to be allowed flourish: they'd a look of things worried by kids and teens and dogs.

'I'm–'

'I know who you are,' Beth says bluntly, her hand at the throat of her tracksuit top. 'I heard you were back.'

'Can I come in?'

'For what?'

'We need to talk.'

She is a thin, waspish-looking woman, dressed in a grey baggy tracksuit, with an unhealthy mole on the nub of her chin. Dark circles cloud her eyes.

'About?' she says. Arms crossed.

He gives her a look that poses a silent question – *are you serious?*

'I think you know,' he says.

She opens the door fully and points to the sitting room. Inside, he waits by the coffee table for her to join him. She has, he realises, gone on down into the kitchen – perhaps to advise those there not to disturb her for the next while.

The room has recently been decorated. Football trophies line the mantel, photographs of a football team are perched on top of a corner cabinet that has empty glass shelves underneath.

A plasma TV needs a spray and a wipe-down. The suite of furniture has a smell of newness. He stands with his back to the fireplace, waiting.

He sits, when silently bidden, in the armchair across from the one she had taken. She sits on the edge, like an anxious gull on a cliff ledge, wondering about the possibility of flight.

'Well,' she says, her eyes fixed on the set fire.

'It concerns my wife, Ena.'

She looks at him and says, 'What about her?'

He thinks Beth is putting too much effort into filling her eyes with blankness.

'I'd like you to tell me about the night she was murdered.'

'I wasn't spilling any tears over her demise.'

'Her murder.'

'Her death.'

'I know who owned the car that was parked up from Farrell's on the night she was murdered.'

'And?'

'And this is where you come in – do you know what it was doing there?'

'You think I killed her?'

'No.'

'Who then?'

'That, I don't know for sure. Why don't you tell me?'

She stares hard at him, but he doesn't flinch.

'I know it wasn't Luigi – nor was it Roger Hall or Don Lally … I'm running out of names.'

'Your mother,' she says, her face becoming dark.

Silence.

He becomes aware of the beat of a clock, its drawing of seconds from his well of life.

'Which is why I won't go to the cops,' he says. 'I think she paid someone.'

'Your mother, your own mother.'

'Was she there?'

'In all but name.'

'Were you?'

'I wouldn't have missed it for the world.'

A sudden rush of anger rages up his throat.

'Tell me, ' he demands.

'Everything?' she says, reaching for her lighter.

He says, 'Everything, right…. Right?'

70

Irene sips at the coffee and moves from the counter to the window, pinches aside the curtain and stares at the rain falling heavily on the street – the drains are streams, choking and gurgling at the shores – people hurrying, a wet dog, head bent over, white and brown coat soaked. She recalls a terrible news bulletin a few years back, of flash flooding in an English town, of a man who'd caught his foot in a storm drain and couldn't free it. The waters were rising and the rescue workers, try as they did, couldn't help. The man drowned. That was tough on everyone, the man, his family, and the men who'd fought desperately to save him.

At the first roll of thunder, she drops the curtain. Lightning crackles. She feels like those rescuers waiting, waiting to see if Dan drowns, if they would manage to free him in time.

71

I met Hazel Rochford and Gilly Maher at Han Kelly's funeral. Han had a heart attack behind the counter in Luigi's – I heard the side of her face fell into the chipper oil. I hoped it wasn't true. I felt a little guilty as I stood at the back of the mourners because I'd met her a couple of times on the street and blanked her. Gilly Maher had married Sny and she was six weeks pregnant, she said. She'd miscarried the other. I was out of the loop and didn't know. Hazel was going to university. She wanted to be a teacher and travel the world. Full of her own shite, as usual.

'How are you doing?' Gilly asked.

It was drizzling, and we were leaving the cemetery before the rain turned heavy.

'Who is she doing, you mean?' Hazel said.

Last time round, I said to her, it was Gilly who'd insulted me in that way. See – kar-fucking-ma. I also felt like slapping the makeup off her chubby face, but instead gripped hard on my packet of smokes and cigarette lighter in separate pockets of my jacket.

'I'm getting married,' I said.

'To Dan! Oh really?' Gilly said, genuinely happy and pleased for me.

Hazel said nothing. Being the bitch.

'Yeah. We're going to get the ring on Saturday, in Lawrence's – it's where Mammy got hers.'

'And look how that worked out,' Hazel said.

Gilly snapped, 'Shut it, Hazel.'

'Miss Perfect,' I said.

'Are you ...' Gilly said.

'No.'

I was, but I amn't now.

'Using the pill or the johnnies?' Hazel asked.

I looked at her to see if she'd heard my warning.

'Both,' I said. 'The pill to ease my periods – the doc prescribed them – and the johnnies to be sure to be sure....'

The pill, after the last scare.

'I see his mother sold her car,' Gilly said.

'Did she?' I said.

'Yeah,' Gilly said, 'my oul fella made her an offer but she said she'd gotten a better one.'

But, Dan said his mother was giving him the car for his birthday. A lovely hardly driven blue Ford Cortina with a black trim. Dan said he had a full licence and planned to drive us to Killarney for our wedding. I'd wanted to visit London instead, or anywhere in England, because I always had a notion to go there. Briefly considered following Young Benny, but wasn't brave enough at the time. Besides, he didn't ask me along.

As Dan pointed out, though, 'You've only been in three of Ireland's counties: Dublin, Kildare and Wicklow. It would be nice for you to see some of your home country before seeing another ... and anyway, we can't afford London.'

He was working full-time in a turf accountant's, having quit college.

'I'd love a car,' Gilly said.

'So would I,' Hazel said, 'a sports car.'

'I'd like a camper van,' I said. 'The idea of driving around with my bed behind me appeals....'

'It'd be handy for you,' Hazel said.

This time, I belted her one. And but for Gilly stepping in, I'd have belted her some more.

He was waiting that evening outside the cinema, looking dejected, like he had all of the town's mad oul ones on his shoulders, and not just his mother.

'Why the face? I said.

'Nothing,' he replied.

I'd told enough lies in my time to be able to spot one a mile off.

We were saving money, so we went to O'Leary's for a drink and a packet of crisps. I was worried about seeing Kevin and Roger, because, apart from watching me, they were watching each other like hawks eyeing up the same prize.

'So, are you going to tell me what's the matter with you – and don't say nothing.'

We were sitting in a small alcove at the front of the pub. A bonsai tree on the sill looked parched. There was a stain in the blind and the cord knot was black from overuse.

'Mam – she sold the car,' he said.

'I know. Gilly told me this morning at Han's funeral.'

'Why didn't you say?'

'I was waiting for you to tell me.'

'Hmm,' he said, then sipped at his lager.

'So, is she giving you the money instead? We can put it towards the wedding.'

He shook his head and said, 'Nope.'

'Nope is what they say in the fucking cowboy films you watch,' I said.

His eyes misted. To distract himself, he started to toy with a beermat.

'I thought the car was yours,' I said.

'So did I.'

'Didn't you say anything to her?'

'Yes.'

'And?'

He was reluctant to say.

'It's me,' I said for him.

Molly had gone berserk when he'd quit college, berserker when he announced that we were getting engaged.

'She threw me out,' he said evenly, with a give to a terrible depth in his voice.

'She what?'

'You heard.'

What's more, if he wanted back in, he was to get shut of me. Fuming, I stood up. A small voice in my head told me she was right – she was protecting her son. I wasn't being faithful to him. I didn't love him.

'I can stay with you and your mam,' he said.

'Sure, of course,' I said, nearly swallowing my teeth thinking on what Mammy would say.

I went and rang Molly from the pub and she hung up. And then I told Dan I'd to meet with Gilly for a bit, and he was to wait in the pub until I came back.

I stormed to Molly's with my blood boiling and hammered on her door. Dan's sister opened up and I brushed by her and marched into the kitchen where Molly was sitting watching TV.

F Troop. Mammy loved that too. Meant to be a comedy, it was. Dry as cactus.

'What's your fucking problem?' I screamed.

Teresa breezed in and told me to get out before she called the police.

'Call who you fucking well like!'

Molly stood, her knee cracked, and said, 'I want you out of my house this second.'

Teresa said, moving to her mother's side, 'Our fucking problem, as you put it, is with him quitting college, and you.'

'You,' Molly said, temper colouring her cheek veins, 'and that Benny Foster – we heard – and about you stealing Luigi's money and your mother's too. My son is way too good for your sort.'

'Listen here, he's the one who did all of the chasing. What do you mean by my sort?'

I knew, but I wanted to hear her say it. Things said give a licence to action, I think. The problem with big people is that they're always surprised when little people kick their shit back, and of the strength that's in their kick.

Teresa said, 'Someone who has no future, nothing going for them. That's your sort.'

'A low-life,' his mother added.

The bitterness and hatred in her tone scorched me deep inside – I could have killed her if I'd stayed, so I left.

'You went where?' Dan said, back in the pub.

'The cow's.'

'Don't call her that.'

'She called me worse.'

'She's–'

'I know what she is.'

'Please….'

'Oh shut the fuck up, will you?'

Nine weeks later, we were married, had moved out of Mammy's to a large but dingy flat down Firecastle Lane, off the market square. So depressing. It was like living in a cave.

From the front door, you could almost reach out a hand and touch the high cathedral wall.

There was always a smell, as if something had died and was rotting away under the floorboards, and the windows were so ridiculously small – a fart wouldn't pass through.

It was the King Kip of kips.

Kevin kept his distance. But Roger Hall was a different story. His quick and sharp glances told me he was waiting for an opportunity. And I was scared he would blurt out things to Dan.

So, I quit the pub, and the week before I got married, your highness in the chemist said she'd to make me redundant.

None of his family came to the wedding and the engagement ring from Lawrence's went by the by. I had to make do with something much cheaper – something that looked like it was taken from a Halloween barmbrack. We'd to go on a harmless pre-marriage course too, and the priest was impressed by the fact that I wasn't pregnant – that we wanted to get married for love. I really liked Dan, but love was a deal off a full measure. I wanted out of the life I was leading. should have gone to England. I could have left behind the nightmares.

Dan wanted to know how I could lie to a priest and I looked at him and said, 'I wasn't lying.'

'You're not pregnant....'

'No. Not anymore. I lost it.'

'Why....'

'Does it matter? Did I need to be pregnant for you to marry me?'

'No ... but you should have told me. It ... it was our baby, not just yours.'

'I was afraid you'd leave me,' I said, which was partly true.

'I wouldn't have,' he said, taking my hand.

At the reception at a place called The Midland Inn I danced the first and last dance with Dan. In between I'd danced with my brother and sister, danced with Harry Wolfe who had taken up with Mammy again, Kevin too and Roger

Hall, who squeezed me tight. If I hadn't invited them, Dan would have asked why not – so I gave an open invitation to the boss, staff and customers. They gave us good presents, I'll say that for them. Enough fucking clocks....

Hazel got drunk and Gilly came without Sny and sat the evening long at her table, listening to the band, and looking terribly unhappy. Mammy said her face would land a job as a tombstone.

72

'You were right,' he says to Irene when she calls, 'about the car.'

'It brought you to a solution?'

'Yes.'

'Blue?'

'A-ha.'

'See?'

'Yeah.'

'So?' she says.

'You mean, what's next?'

'Yes, Dan. What is next?'

Silence.

'Home, perhaps?' she suggests.

'Sounds good, more than good.'

'Oh.'

'And ... another shot, giving me another chance. Would you consider it?'

The plaintive note in his voice cuts her to the quick. She finds it hard to catch her breath with the pain of it. She wants to say the words that she knows he wants to hear, but she knows too much has happened, too much has been said, and too much has been left unsaid for them to ever fix things. She knows she must be brave, for both of them, or else they will destroy each other. 'It's over, done, Dan,' she says, 'your time in Ireland, our time with each other. There's nothing left anymore.'

73

Our honeymoon was in Adare, in a hotel across the road from a row of beautiful cottages, all of which had flowers blooming out front. A friend of his dropped us there and we got a bus back to town two days later. We spent the time arguing. Being broke all of the time does that to people – brings out their bad side. It's good to have some jingle jangle in your bank account.

He hadn't improved any in bed. I mean, God, he wouldn't even try any other position except on top. And he still didn't last too long – on and off in the time it took me to blink. I tried blow jobbing him, but Jesus, he freaked out, saying he didn't like that sort of thing. It wasn't fair on him, because I was more experienced, but....

In the weeks that followed, I was drinking a lot and a fierce thirst seemed to grab hold of me. I got these wild cravings for booze and would go to the pub – not always the same one – when he was at work. I'd see a good-looking man and if there was a little chemistry sizzling between us, the inevitable happened. Then, I started going out in the evenings and after that he began to find out things about me, and believe them. I felt sort of liberated that he was no longer in the dark – I no longer had to pretend. I was his black rose.

He tried talking me into seeing sense and what he called behaving properly – when that didn't work, he tried hitting me, he tried all he could to bring me onside, but I didn't love him enough to try – I didn't love myself enough either.

I often saw Bella Foster in my dreams, about to cross the road, ignoring Mammy and me, and I put out my hand and pushed her in the back. My hand was the wind, the wind my hand.

And it was such a light push. Except in reality, it wasn't a push. No, it was a reaching out, because I realised she wasn't ignoring us, but instead was hanging on to her hat, herself, as the wind was strong. She was terrified. And I put my hand out to grab the belt on the back of her coat, to stop the wind sweeping her off her feet, but I was too slow and my reach never touched her. Out of her brown shoes it stole her, and her blood spattered my face and landed on my tongue. In me, in a swallow. And my perception of the world turned bad, and I was soured.

'England,' he said, minutes after he'd tracked me down. 'You're going to England?'

We were four months married yesterday. He reminded me.

'On what?' he said.

I said nothing.

'A magic carpet?' he said.

'I have money.'

'Where did you get it?'

'I've been saving.'

'How much?'

'About eight hundred.'

Shouldn't have said that, but I wanted to convince him I was serious.

'You've got that much money – and yet the ESB might be cutting off our electricity any day.'

'I'm going to England.'

'Oh, you're going to England. I'm staying, is that the plan?'

'Yes. It's not working out.'

'How could it – you haven't given it a chance, have you?'

I couldn't say that I had.

'Sure, as you said yourself, I'm only a whore.'

'You've a good track record.'

'Why bother with me then?'

'Because,' he said, 'because....'

He couldn't say the word. It wouldn't grow on his lips. *Love.* I picked up my jacket and left.

An hour later, in the Leinster Arms pub, next to the police station, Hazel put her head in and looked around. When she saw me, she came over, helped herself to a chip from my plate and said, 'Have you seen the state of Gilly?'

'No,' I said.

'He bet the living shit out of her,' she said.

'Who did?'

'Sny.'

'The bastard.'

'He's going to kill her,' Hazel said, 'he fucking will.'

I told her to have a chip. Her eyes were a hawk's on them.

'I'm trying to get a few quid together to get her to her sister in England,' she said.

'Whereabouts?'

'Leeds, I think.'

She dipped a chip in ketchup and said, 'You should see the state of her.'

I did. A little later, in Hazel's kitchen. Two black eyes, one shut, a broken front tooth, and a bite mark on her arm. It was the first time I'd cried in a while. Sny was a higher grade of bastard than Roger Hall, and that was saying something.

'I'll go with you,' I said.

Gilly looked at me and said, 'Would you, really?'

'I said I would. I've got money for the fares and enough to tide us over....'

Mammy's money, five hundred of it – that I'd borrowed for the wedding but held back and the rest from Kevin and Luigi, who said he would have given me more, but I owed him five hundred. He said it as if I'd stolen his soul.

'Tomorrow,' I said, 'in the evening.'

I was thinking that Kevin might give me some sympathy money when I told him about Sny and his antics. I'll be back, I intended saying to him, just seeing that she gets over okay.

I didn't drink much in the pub at his birthday party, and he gave me fifty quid to help with Gilly's cause. When he was drunk he told people where I was going. Then he invited us down to his place – Poncho McDonagh was camping close-by and he'd suspected the McDonaghs of stealing tarpaulin and building material. So we went and it was a great party and everyone sang a party-piece. I sang what words I knew of 'The White Rose of Athens'.

Mammy was there for a little and then mooched off with a neighbour in a taxi, and that Beth bitch and Young Benny, who had to fix his eyes in every direction except mine. He was terrified Beth might catch him eyeing me up – which I knew he really wanted to do. She was looking at him to snare him looking at me, and I was breaking my arse laughing at him, because he so much wanted to look. Then she left, and others started dribbling away and I was the last in the house. I couldn't sleep. I had to go pack a case and get to the bank early to change currency.

Kevin was snoring. Drooling onto his pillow. His wallet was on the table and I considered raiding it. I could be trusted with money but not with a man's heart – a deep sadness weighed on my shoulders as I went down his stairs and let myself out.

It was a beautiful clear night. I watched the stars and lit up a cigarette, wishing I hadn't to face into the walk to Mammy's. No taxi at this hour. I saw Luigi's car and wondered why the hell he'd come back after dropping off the other lads. He was mouldy. I went over and said through the open window, 'If the cops see you you'll be in shit.'

'Get in,' he said.

'I'll walk, if you don't mind.'

'I do fucking mind, Ena.'

'Fuck off will you, Jesus … men.'

'I have something … to tell you … they're coming for you … I overheard her … Benny and your one, Beth, he's coming for you.'

'Yeah, go home … just go home. Better still, head into Kevin's place and sleep it off.'

I walked on. I heard the car door open, close, and turned and said, 'Would you ever get a life, would you? Look at the state of you. For God's sake. Really. Fuck sake.'

He came up to me. I could smell the vodka from him, see its mist in his eyes.

'You fucking owe me big-time,' he said. 'I gave you a job – I let you rob me blind, eat my food.'

'I'll pay you back.'

'When? You're leaving the … fucking country.'

I shook my head. Asked myself if this was really happening.

'But…' he said.

This leer filled his face. He touched my breast and I slapped his face – he came back with an instinctive slap, strong. I fell. Struck my head against a brick or something. It hurt like nothing I'd ever felt before. He helped me to my feet, gushing sorries. I stood wavering from side to side. He saying to forget the money, forget it, and write it off. When he took his hands away, I sank hard to the ground with him hanging out of me, calling my name.

74

Beth told him that yeah, she'd gone down in the car to confront Ena about giving her Benny the come on at Kevin's party. She got a lift back down with a man who'd also wanted to see Ena. But when they arrived there, she wouldn't get out of the car.

'I got very afraid,' she'd said.

'Do you remember the night?' he'd said. 'Clearly remember?'

'I'd drink on me, but I sobered up pretty quickly. The man with me – this is how clear it is to me – he wore a greyish jumper. It smelled of fabric conditioner. He had a long lean face that was meaner than I'd ever seen it. It was as though something in his skull had tightened the flesh in his face. His lips, I couldn't see them, his wrinkles were pronounced, and his eyes sparkled with intent.

'Who was he?'

She inhaled and then said, 'My father, Owen Noctor.'

'Him?'

'Yes … and here's what I'm going to tell you, Mister Somers, when we got there, your wife was already lying on the grass, off the road a little. Our headlights showed her – so my dad got out and went over and he kneeled down beside her and then he moved her further onto the grassland, so she wouldn't be seen. He came back and said she was done for … someone saved us a job.'

'You left her there … she was alive. Jesus.'

'He thought she was dead. And I think he really believed she was.'

'Why move her?'

'Because he wanted to be well away before she was found … that's what he said.'

Tears filled his eyes. His hands got the tremors.

She left him alone, and after some minutes he let himself out.

His mother, he now knows, had given Noctor the car in exchange for his chasing Ena out of her son's life. A hard and cruel man, Beth's father had a history of being a tough character: a debt collector, a bouncer. He was forty-two years old at the time. Guilt-stricken, Dan's mother later changed her will to include him once more. Within weeks his mother was dead. Ena was leaving him anyway – but his mother hadn't known that – if a broken heart could bring you to your grave, so too could immeasurable regret.

Owen Noctor took the ferry with *his* car to England the next morning, neglecting to tell Dan's mother he hadn't earned his fee. Ena lay unconscious for most of the day, till Poncho McDonagh came across her in the furze and raised the alarm.

He has found the answers and yet he understands that the dance Irene spoke of is not over, and perhaps will never end. He does not know for sure who killed his wife. He now only knows who did not. And he is not much wiser for having tried his hardest.

75

I heard his voice and felt his touch and I could not respond to it, except through a tear, which I hoped he might see and understand for what it was – a goodbye, a recognition of his love for me, and a deep sorrow. I had not been able to give him my heart, no matter how much I wanted to … I simply had nothing in me to give. The wind stole the best part of me, and no one saw the theft.